Dear Reader:

LOVESWEPT celebrates heroes, those irresistible men who sweep us off our feet, who tantalize us with whispered endearments, and who challenge us with their teasing humor and hidden vulnerability. Whether they're sexy roughnecks or dashing sophisticates, dark and dangerous or blond and brash, these men are heartthrobs, the kind no woman can get enough of. And now, just in time for Valentine's Day, all six books in this month's line-up have truly special covers that feature only these gorgeous heartthrobs. HEARTTHROBS—heroes who'll leave you spellbound as only real men can, in six fabulous new romances by only the best in the genre.

**Don't miss any of our HEARTTHROBS this month**

#528 A MAGNIFICENT AFFAIR by Fayrene Preston
#529 CALL ME SIN by Jan Hudson
#530 MR. PERFECT by Doris Parmett
#531 LOVE AND A BLUE-EYED COWBOY
    by Sandra Chastain
#532 TAKEN BY STORM by Tami Hoag
#532 BRANDED by Linda Warren

There's no better way to celebrate the most romantic day of the year than to cuddle up with all six LOVESWEPT HEARTTHROBS!

With best wishes,

*Nita Taublib*

Nita Taublib
Associate Publisher/LOVESWEPT

## WHAT ARE *LOVESWEPT* ROMANCES?

They are stories of true romance and touching emotion. We believe those two very important ingredients are constants in our highly sensual and very believable stories in the *LOVESWEPT* line. Our goal is to give you, the reader, stories of consistently high quality that may sometimes make you laugh, sometimes make you cry, but are always fresh and creative and contain many delightful surprises within their pages.

Most romance fans read an enormous number of books. Those they truly love, they keep. Others may be traded with friends and soon forgotten. We hope that each *LOVESWEPT* romance will be a treasure—a "keeper." We will always try to publish

*LOVE STORIES YOU'LL NEVER FORGET*
*BY AUTHORS YOU'LL ALWAYS REMEMBER*

The Editors

*Loveswept* ® 528

## Fayrene Preston
## A Magnificent Affair

**BANTAM BOOKS**
NEW YORK · TORONTO · LONDON · SYDNEY · AUCKLAND

A MAGNIFICENT AFFAIR

*A Bantam Book / March 1992*

*If you would be interested in receiving protective vinyl
covers for your Loveswept books, please write to this address
for information:*

*Loveswept
Bantam Books
P.O. Box 985
Hicksville, NY 11802*

ISBN 0-553-44170-1

*Published simultaneously in the United States and Canada*

*Bantam Books are published by Bantam Books, a division
of Bantam Doubleday Dell Publishing Group, Inc. Its trademark, consisting of the words "Bantam Books" and the
portrayal of a rooster, is Registered in U.S. Patent and
Trademark Office and in other countries. Marca Registrada.
Bantam Books, 666 Fifth Avenue, New York, New York 10103.*

PRINTED IN THE UNITED STATES OF AMERICA

OPM    0 9 8 7 6 5 4 3 2 1

# One

Max Hayden strode across the empty lobby of his inn, heading toward the stairs. "I'm going up, Cameron."

Cameron grinned. In his early twenties, the inn's night manager stood behind the old, battered teakwood bar that served as the reception desk. "Going to finish that Stephen King book tonight, boss?"

"I plan to."

"Let's see"—Cameron checked his watch—"it's almost midnight. Want me to send someone up to check on you in a couple of hours, just in case the book scares you to death?"

Max chuckled. "That won't be necessary. There are very few things in life that scare me."

Just then, he heard the sounds of a car skidding to a stop with a crunch of gravel, a muted thud, and the crash of something breaking.

With his foot on the first step of the stairs, Max

glanced at Cameron. "You'd better go see what's happened."

"I hope no one's hurt," Cameron said, rounding the desk.

Following his long-standing practice of letting his staff handle all routine aspects of running the inn, Max continued up the stairs. "Let me know if you need me."

Cameron reached the front door and pulled it open just in time for a young woman to lurch through the doorway, holding the root ball of a geranium in one hand and a Louis Vuitton suitcase in the other.

"The pot is on the critical list," she said, slightly breathless, "but the geranium will pull through." Her lovely green eyes glimmered with friendliness, but were shadowed with fatigue. She glanced at his name tag. "Do people call you Cam?"

From his position at the top of the stairs, Max didn't hear Cameron's reply. All his attention was riveted on her.

Her voice had made him stop. It was warm, soft, with an innocent seductiveness. Then he had turned and seen her. Intrigued, he had remained.

She was tall, with long, slender legs and delectable curves that were shown off to spectacular advantage in a three-hundred dollar pair of designer jeans and a fifteen-dollar souvenir T-shirt emblazoned with a map of Montana. Her hair was the color of a fine burgundy wine and hung half in and half out of a long braid. Cameron, he noticed, couldn't seem to take his eyes off her, and he understood why.

"I'm Ashley Whitfield," she said, "but call me

Ashley. I can't *tell* you how glad I am to finally be here." She handed him the geranium. "I'm afraid the pot is in pieces on the driveway, but the geranium will live if you replant it. You will replant it, won't you? Promise me you'll replant it."

"Ah . . . I'll make sure our gardener does."

"Good. Naturally I'll pay for the new pot, plus the post I hit. Just let me know how much . . ." Her voice died as her mind switched gears and she noticed her surroundings. Polished oak floors, sisal area rugs, nautical-theme paintings, comfortable furnishings, and brass light fixtures greeted her tired eyes. Her first impression was that the inn offered peace and refuge, two things she was in desperate need of. She smiled at Cameron. "This is wonderful, but then an inn called the Place of Happiness couldn't be anything less than fantastic. Right?"

"May I help you with your bag?" Cameron asked.

"No, thanks. I can handle it." She transferred her bag from one hand to the other, and the locks opened, the entire contents of the suitcase spilling onto the gleaming oak floor. With a disgusted scowl she gazed down at the rainbow of silken lingerie punctuated by an assortment of shoes, clothing, and a hair dryer.

Cameron was at her side at once. "Let me help you."

She sighed and dropped the Louis Vuitton bag to the floor as if it were a paper sack. "Don't worry about it, I'll pick it up in a minute. For now let's just get me checked in." She rubbed her back, then proceeded to the reservation desk. "I'm exhausted. I've been driving *days* to get here. I can't tell you exactly how many days it's been since I left New York, but it's been a lot."

Cameron hurried around the desk and worriedly gazed at her. "You don't have a reservation, do you?"

She rewarded his perceptiveness with a smile that lit up her whole face. "No."

Cameron stared at her, his expression one of rapt fascination.

"You see, I have this bothersome tendency to get lost. I have no sense of direction, and I've never been able to acquire one." She shrugged. "I even have a compass in my car, but it keeps turning, and I can't bring myself to trust it. I mean, what if *it's* wrong? I'm certain compasses aren't infallible. Very few things in life are, don't you agree? Anyway, I wasn't sure how long it would take me to get here, and it would have been unfair of me to ask you to hold a room for me when I couldn't tell you the exact date I would be arriving." She took a breath. "You understand, don't you?"

Transfixed, Cameron managed to nod. "I understand completely."

"I was sure you would."

"Yes, but . . . I hate to tell you this, but I'm afraid we're all booked up." With apparent anxiety over his inability to give her a room, Cameron wrung his hands together. "We usually are on weekends."

She looked at him blankly. "Weekends?"

"It's Saturday night," he said gently.

"I didn't realize . . . I think I was in Ohio when I lost track of the days."

"Ohio?"

She wiped a hand over her face. "Maybe it was Iowa. That's where I took the wrong turn. Or, at any rate, the last *big* wrong turn." She gnawed on her bottom lip, thinking that she was almost positive it had been Iowa. She had visited a pre-historic Indian burial site there. . . . Her mind switched gears again as an odd thing happened. The air along her right side seemed to turn several degrees warmer. Curious, she looked in the direction of the warmth and saw a man standing there. He had blue eyes that penetrated her weariness and awakened her senses and chiseled features that made her completely lose her train of thought. There was only one thing she could think of to say. "Hi."

He gave a slight nod.

As he continued to remain silent, her brow pleated. There seemed to be no reason for his sudden appearance, but then she had never been overly bothered by things that didn't make sense. She turned back to Cameron. "There's got to be some place here I can sleep tonight. A broom closet, a corner of the kitchen, maybe an elevator you don't use too often. . . ."

He shook his head with regret. "I'm afraid not. But if you go back out to the main road and drive south, you'll find several hotels and motels—"

"No, that won't work. I'd like to tell you it would, but it won't, so I can't. I'd never be able to find them."

"I'd be happy to draw you a map."

"It wouldn't help." She reached across the desk and covered his hand with hers in a confiding manner. "You're going to have to trust me on this.

I'd end up in Alaska. Not that I don't want to see Alaska one day. I do. In fact, I think at one point during this trip I was just a few miles from the border, but—" She saw Cameron's eyes cut to the man at her right. She also looked toward the man, just in time to see him nod.

Cameron cleared his throat. "It turns out we do have one room we can let you have."

"Really?" Ashley gazed at the blue-eyed man. "Thank you." She paused and considered the matter. "What exactly am I thanking you for? You're not giving up your room, are you, because I couldn't let you do that."

With another look at the man Cameron spoke up. "No, it's a room on the third floor that's kept for special guests. As it happens, no one's staying there now, and you're welcome to use it until another room opens up."

"That's very kind of you," she told the man even though he hadn't said a word. There was probably something significant here she should grasp, she thought. And she was vaguely aware of the urge to comb her hair and put on some lipstick. He was so wildly attractive. . . . But all in all she was too tired to care or to question.

Abruptly he strode over to the suitcase, dropped to a knee, and began putting her clothes back in.

She followed and came down beside him. "Please don't bother with this. I'm used to cleaning up my own messes, and I can manage."

He held up an emerald-green silk teddy and gazed straight into her eyes, silencing her. "Pretty."

Slightly bemused by the sight of her undergarment dangling from his big hand, she took the teddy from him. "Thanks." Even as tired as she was, she didn't have to wonder why she found him so compelling. He reeked of a sexuality and masculinity that seemed to her as powerful as a force of nature. Just being near him had her tingling from the top of her head to the soles of her feet. But she just got out of the frying pan. She had no intention of jumping into the fire.

Carefully, competently, he folded another teddy and neatly placed it in the suitcase.

He seemed quite accustomed to handling feminine undergarments, she thought, grasping several chemises and shoving them into the suitcase. "Look, don't worry about being neat. I never do. I've always felt that spending a lot of time packing is a huge waste of time. I mean, you just have to unpack again at the end of the trip. Don't you agree?" She didn't actually expect him to agree with her—it was a rare occurrence when someone did—but she had expected some sort of response. There was nothing. She gazed at him through her thick lashes. "You don't talk a lot, do you?"

"The contents of your suitcase make it look like a lingerie shop."

She would rather he had commented on the weather than on her wardrobe of intimate garments, but at least he had spoken a complete sentence. "Yeah, well, I never know what color I'm going to want to wear on what particular day, so I buy all the colors." It rarely bothered her to explain things about herself. People always seemed to be questioning one aspect of her life or another. "I love vivid colors, don't you?"

It would be easy to grow attached to *her* vivid coloring, he thought. He had never known that wine-red hair could make him want to wrap himself in its silky strands. And he had never known that he could be so intrigued by green eyes that were shadowed with fatigue, along with something else that wasn't so easy to read.

He fingered a pair of royal-blue tap pants; a light but definitely sensual scent drifted up from the fabric. From the corner of his eyes he saw Cameron hovering. "Is this all your luggage?" he asked her.

"No. The rest is in the Mercedes out front, the one that looks as if it's trying to climb the steps of the inn."

"Cameron."

"Right away." The tone of his voice clearly expressed regret that he was going to have to leave the interesting scene. "Do you have your keys, Miss Whitfield?"

"Call me Ashley. And the keys are still in the car. Oh, and you'd better take a cart. Besides the suitcases, there are several boxes in the backseat with souvenirs I've bought on the trip. I tried to keep them organized, like using one box per section of the country, but I'm afraid I kept forgetting which box was which. Be especially careful of the Indian headdress."

She could only imagine her mother's reaction to the headdress, not to mention the assortment of ashtrays and candlesticks, though she knew her mother would temper her reaction by finding something positive to say about them. Her mother had always been loving and supportive, quick to praise her smallest accomplishments. There was no doubt in Ashley's mind that her mother wanted her happiness. Unfortunately her mother's definition of happiness didn't agree with her own. Roger was a prime example of that.

Frowning, she picked up a T-shirt that bore the words NOTHING WITHOUT PROVIDENCE. She turned it so that he could see the slogan. "Is this California's state motto?"

"No."

"Then it must be Colorado's motto." She tossed it into the suitcase.

"Are you staying long?"

"I plan to. I hope to. But then again, I'm not entirely sure." She shrugged. "My plans have a habit of changing themselves."

"Why is that?"

"I don't honestly know. My father says the reason nothing holds my attention for very long is because I'm so bright I get bored easily. My mother says it's because I have a short attention span and get preoccupied with other things."

"What do you think?"

No one had ever asked her that before. "They're probably both right, but personally I wish they wouldn't worry about it so much."

He stared at her for a moment, then glanced down at her hand. Was there a faint impression on the third finger of her left hand where a ring had been? He wouldn't be surprised. He couldn't imagine this vivid creature unattached. She was made for a man to make love to. "Are you traveling alone?"

"Yes."

Gold streaks radiated out from her pupils, creating a star formation. Unable to help himself, he reached out to brush a thick lock of hair from her eyes and anchor it behind her ear. His fingertips lingered on her, trailing down her throat and up under her chin to cup it. "Did anyone ever tell you that you have stars in your eyes?"

His touch heated her entire body, and she felt as if she were in danger of dissolving on the spot. She tried hard to convince herself it was because she was tired. She was not successful. "My eyes are a little strange, aren't they?"

"I didn't say that."

She swallowed. "I wonder if you would mind taking your hand off me. You see, you have the strangest effect on me, and I'm just not up to it right now."

He slowly smiled. "You say everything you think, don't you?"

Her pulse was racing, making it difficult for her to know exactly *what* she was thinking. "Not everything. At least I try not to, but yes, I guess I do. Sometimes. Especially when I'm tired . . . or nervous."

"What do you have to be nervous about?"

"You."

He stared at her. "Saying everything you think could be dangerous."

"I know," she said softly, meeting his steady gaze. "It can also be quite embarrassing. I'll work on it, I promise."

He released her and lifted a ruby-red lace bra by its strap. She grabbed it from him and thrust it into the suitcase.

She would look like sex personified in that bra, he thought, feeling his stomach knot. His wanting her was an immediate, pulsating shock to his system. And it made him extremely uneasy. He bunched his muscles to rise, then saw the matching panties lying by his knee on the floor. His long fingers closed around them, savoring the feel of the handful of silk. What would an armful of her feel like? he wondered.

He had the most absurd urge to bury his face in the panties and inhale its scent. He almost did. Until he caught himself.

*Following impulses could also be dangerous.*

Without looking at her, he quickly scooped the rest of her things into the suitcase and snapped it closed.

A second later both locks opened again.

Ashley glanced at him and saw that he was staring in bewilderment at the locks. "I don't know what the problem is. The locks have been acting temperamental since Memphis. I probably should have bought a roll of strapping tape while I was there, but I went to Graceland instead. Have you ever been there? Lovely place."

His piercing gaze shifted to her.

Cameron returned, rolling the luggage cart in front of him. Max surged to his feet, and holding the suitcase closed, he placed it on the cart. "Be careful of that one. The lock's broken."

Cameron nodded and looked at Ashley. "I parked your car for you. By the way, it doesn't look as if it was damaged."

"I wasn't worried."

No, Max thought. She had been more worried

about the geranium than her Mercedes, or the fact that she was waltzing into a popular weekend getaway spot without a reservation and without even knowing what day it was.

"Are you ready to go up to your room?" Cameron asked her.

"Yes." She turned toward the man. "Thank you for helping me with my bag. I really appreciate it."

"No problem," he said, knowing he was lying. If ever he had seen a problem, she was it.

He folded his arms across his chest and watched as she and Cameron disappeared into the elevator.

Only minutes earlier he had told Cameron that there were very few things in life that scared him. But he might have just come face-to-face with one of those things.

*Ashley.*

It wasn't as if she had done anything alarming. On the contrary, she had been pleasant and friendly. But, dammit, she bothered him. Despite being tired, despite the enigmatic shadows in her eyes, she was upbeat, quirky, direct, and with a beauty that nettled him.

What's more, she didn't seem to fit into any category of woman he'd ever known.

His gut instinct told him she came with invisible strings that were capable of reaching out to a man and binding him to her so securely he might never escape. She made a man want to bring her into his life, take care of those puzzling shadows in her eyes, and make sure she never lost her way again.

He had carefully fashioned his life. He got up when he wanted to; he went to bed when he wanted to. If at a moment's notice he wanted to take off to Australia for deep-sea fishing, he did. If he wanted to go to Africa for a photographic safari, he didn't have to consult anyone. He had no desire to be tied to one place or one woman.

No one would ever call him a coward, but why tempt fate? He knew himself and what he wanted, and he intended to steer completely clear of Ashley Whitfield. In fact, now might be a good time to take the boat down to Cabo San Lucas. . . .

Ashley awakened with a smile on her face to the unfamiliar sound of the ocean. It was a much better sound to wake up to than New York traffic, she decided.

The previous night she had taken a bath to loosen her stiff muscles, and had almost fallen asleep in the tub. After she finally went to bed, she had slept deeply and had dreams she couldn't remember now. But the dreams didn't matter. She had gotten a good night's rest and felt terrific.

A glance at the bedside clock told her it was 8:00 A.M. The sun streaming through the open French doors of her room told her it was already a glorious day.

She stretched, then slid out of bed and headed for the bathroom. A few minutes later she was back in the bedroom, her face washed, her teeth brushed. And craving her first-thing-in-the-morning Coke.

She snatched up the ice bucket and left her room. Several steps later it dawned on her that she had gone in the wrong direction. She was out on the balcony instead of in the hallway. What's more, she had forgotten to put on a robe.

With a sigh of resignation she started back to her room, but the sound of a phone ringing nearby stopped her. Heavens, but she *hated* the sound of a ringing phone.

Her brow creased with annoyance, and she glanced in the direction of the irritating sound. Farther along the balcony, a set of French doors stood open. Obviously no one was in there, she reasoned, or someone would have answered the phone by now. Either that or the occupant was dead. She frowned as she contemplated this far from cheerful thought.

All the while the phone kept ringing, and each ring was like nails across a chalkboard to her. The caller wasn't going to give up. With an exclamation she went to answer it.

*She wasn't alone.* The realization brought her to a standstill several feet inside the room. A man was sleeping soundly on the king-sized bed. He lay sprawled on his stomach, a pillow over his head. His only other covering was a sheet that rested just below his waist and molded over his hips. His right leg had escaped the sheet.

She stared uncertainly at him. Judging by the even rise and fall of his back, he appeared to be breathing. That was definitely a plus. But who in the world could sleep through the shrill ringing of a telephone?

The phone rang again. And again. And her nerves jangled with each ring. *She had to stop that noise.*

"Excuse me," she said to the sleeping man. "Your

phone is ringing." No response. "Do you want me to answer your phone?" Still no response. "Okay, then," she said to him, just to make the whole thing official, "I'll answer your phone and take a message for you." She rounded the bed on tiptoes and snatched up the receiver.

"Hello," she whispered. Even though the man was lying on the other side of the bed, she could actually feel the heat of his body on her skin. Still, she felt safe. If a ringing phone couldn't wake him up, the sound of her voice certainly wouldn't.

"Is Max there?" a vaguely familiar female voice asked.

Ashley glanced at the sleeping figure, and her eyes fell on the corded muscles ridging his back. "I'm not sure."

"Offhand I wouldn't think this was a difficult question." The voice sounded amused. "Either he is or he isn't."

"Well, you're right about that," Ashley said, still gazing at the athletic form. Even though he was asleep and she couldn't see his face, she received the overwhelming impression of sexuality. What was it about this place? she wondered. She hadn't been here but a few hours, and already she had met two sexy men.

Well, she silently amended, she hadn't actually *met* either of them.

"Hello? Are you still there?"

"Oh. Yes, I'm here, and there is also very definitely a man here. It's just that I don't know who he is. But don't worry. If you think you dialed the right number, and the number is your friend

Max's room, then I would think there's a pretty good chance his name is Max."

"Let me get this straight. You're in his room, and you don't know his name?"

"Yeah, that's pretty much it. You see, I can't stand the sound of a phone that rings on and on, so I thought—"

"What's he doing?"

"Doing? He's sleeping. Deep. In fact, I've never seen anyone sleep this deep. Personally I can't understand how anyone can sleep through a ringing phone."

The person on the other end of the line sighed. "Look, wake him up for me, will you? I need to talk to him."

The idea of reaching out and touching him—his warm, sleek skin, his muscles that would ripple when he moved—had her feeling weak and light-headed. She *really* needed that Coke. "I've already tried to wake him up. I talked to him and everything. I think it would be better if you gave me a message instead, and I'll leave it some place where he can't miss it."

"Oh, all right. This is Ginnie Averone."

"*Ginnie!*" In her excitement, she sank onto the bed, holding the ice bucket against her. "Ginnie, it's me, Ashley."

"*Ashley!* I *thought* your voice sounded familiar."

"I thought yours did too, but I couldn't be sure because I haven't had my morning Coke yet." She crossed her legs, Indian-fashion. "How are you?"

"I'm fine. And you're the reason I was phoning Max. Your mother called me yesterday, worried. She expected to hear from you days ago."

Ashley noticed an open Stephen King book on the pillow in front of her, along with a pair of glasses. "You didn't tell her where I was heading, did you?"

"Yes. I had to. She was threatening to notify the FBI."

"Yeah, well, she tends to overreact at times."

"I was beginning to get worried about you, too, Ashley. Why haven't you checked in?"

"I just arrived last night. I took a few wrong turns."

"Oh."

Ashley put down the ice bucket, picked up the glasses, and looked through them, squinting. The vision correction wasn't too bad, she decided. They must be reading glasses.

"Well, honey, you happen to be in Max Hayden's bedroom. How did that come about?"

"I was on my way to the soda machine and decided to answer the phone." She turned her head and gazed at the sleeping man through his glasses. Even blurred, he still looked incredibly sexy. "Who's Max Hayden?"

"He owns the inn. I'm sure I mentioned his name." She paused. "Your room must be on the third floor."

"It is. They were all booked up when I arrived last night, and then this man appeared at my side and nodded to Cameron—he's the young man who was on the desk. Anyway, then Cameron said I could use a room that's reserved for special guests until another one opens up."

"The man who nodded must have been Max."

The glasses slipped from her suddenly numb

fingers. "You mean I'm sitting on the bed of the man who—"

"Who what?"

*Who she had dreamed about.* She remembered now. He had dominated her dreams with those blue eyes of his, and she had heated when he had touched her. "Uh, the man who gave me the room."

"You sure are. And I'm glad he did. I meant to call him sooner and let him know you were coming and that you were a friend of mine. But this pregnancy has sapped all my energy. I keep falling asleep. That is, in between running to the bathroom with morning sickness that lasts all day."

"Gosh, I'm sorry to hear that." Diverted by the subject of her friend's pregnancy, she rested the phone between her ear and her shoulder and idly thumbed through the Stephen King book. "How's Damien handling it all?"

Ginnie laughed. "I'm only three months pregnant, and already he's a candidate for a nervous breakdown. You'd think no woman had ever gotten through a pregnancy successfully before. He's treating me as if I were made out of glass."

"What's wrong with a little pampering? Besides, think about it. Damien must be feeling pretty helpless regarding the whole situation, and pampering you is about the only thing he can do, at least until the baby is born."

Ginnie laughed. "I guess you're right."

Ashley bent closer to the book and read a particularly horrific line. "Your friend Max must have nerves of steel if his reading habits are anything to go by." She turned a few pages and read another line at random.

"Why do you say that?"

"Because—"

*"Don't lose my place."*

Ashley nearly jumped out of her skin. She jerked in the direction of the husky masculine voice and found that the pillow no longer covered his head. More importantly, she was gazing into a pair of deep blue eyes. The eyes in her dreams. The *man* in her dreams. "He's awake," she whispered to Ginnie.

"Good. Put him on."

"Are you Max?" she asked him, still whispering.

He took the phone from her hand. "Ginnie? Hi. I hear Damien's having a bad time of it." He kept his gaze on Ashley as he listened for a minute, then softly chuckled. "Tell him I said it couldn't be happening to a more deserving guy. I can't wait to see him change diapers."

Ashley began to ease off the bed, but his long arm snaked out and his hand clamped around her wrist, keeping her where she was. He listened again. "Yeah, your friend got here. You really should have warned me." He laughed at the answering retort. "Don't worry. If I have to, I'll assign a bodyguard to her and increase my insurance." He laughed again. "Okay, okay, I'll talk to you in a few days. In the meantime, tell Damien hi." He paused. "Okay, 'bye." Still holding her arm, he reached past Ashley and hung up the phone.

Then he turned his attention to her. She was sitting cross-legged on his bed, wearing a short chemise with matching panties made out of sheer watercolor floral-print chiffon. Her hair was a tousled, wine-colored haze around her face and shoulders. Her green eyes were wide and no longer shadowed with fatigue. Her skin was golden beige and gleamed as if it had a satin finish. He had never seen anyone or anything more desirable. So much for steering clear of her.

"Can I help you?"

She stared blankly at him. "Help me?"

"You're in my room, sitting on my bed. I assume there's a logical reason."

"Oh, yes. You see, I needed a Coke, and I heard your phone, and I didn't know you were here, and if you were, there was a good possibility that you were dead, because after all, who could sleep—" Her curiosity sidetracked her. "How on earth can you sleep so soundly? At home, if I can't answer my phone within two rings, my answering machine is set to pick it up."

He released her, rolled over, arranged several pillows into a mound behind him, and maneuvered upward until he was lying back against them. "There aren't too many things that'll wake me up. I'm retired, and I don't generally wake up before ten."

"You miss an awful lot of the morning that way."

"That's the way I like it." His gaze drifted downward. Through the sheer fabric of the chemise, he could see the pointed tips of her breasts, a delicate rose-beige color. And lower on her body, a triangle of dark red hair.

She followed his gaze and gasped. She had completely forgotten what she had on. She made a hasty grab for the sheet, but he was faster and tugged it back to his waist.

"You've got on more clothes than I do, Ashley.

Unless you don't care that I'm naked. If you don't . . ."

She held up a hand. "You're right. You should have the sheet."

"Thank you."

She snatched up the ice bucket and clutched it to her, but she was bolted to the spot by the thought of him naked. Surprising, tantalizing, not to mention highly inappropriate, images danced in her head. *My, oh my.*

"Think frying pan and fire, Ashley," she muttered under her breath.

"Excuse me?"

"Nothing. I've got to go now." She slid off the bed and began backing away. "I'm terribly sorry I woke you up, but I came here for peace, and the incessant sound of your phone ringing was not peaceful. Besides, you know, I figured it must have been important because the caller wouldn't hang up, and as it turns out, the caller was Ginnie. Wasn't that a coincidence?"

His eyes were hooded as he followed her with his gaze.

She reached the French doors. "But, listen, I really am sorry. Why don't you just go back to sleep and forget I was ever here?" She would also try to forget, but she seriously doubted she had that much power over her thoughts. She took a step out onto the balcony. " 'Bye."

Then she remembered something and stuck her head back in. "Is there a soda machine on this floor?"

"*No!*"

She turned and hurried across the balcony to her room.

Max rolled over and buried his head beneath the pillows. What in the hell was wrong with him? His body was hard and aching. He *wanted* her, and he had only touched her wrist.

Dammit. If she had stayed five more seconds, he would have pulled her to him and made love to her until neither one of them could walk.

The woman was dangerous and needed a keeper, but he wanted no part of the job. As soon as he got up, he was going to make plans for heading to Cabo San Lucas.

But the first order of business was a cold shower.

# Two

He felt better, Max told himself, as he strolled across the lobby, politely nodding to the inn's guests, warmly greeting his employees. He relished the feeling of normalcy.

Ashley had taken him off guard, that was all, pulling him out of a deep sleep with her lightly erotic scent and her softly seductive voice. But he was wide awake now, and as soon as he had breakfast, he would go down to the marina and begin to ready his boat for the trip.

He turned the corner into the dining room and came to a dead stop. Ashley was sitting at his table.

"What is she doing at my table?" he asked Bill, a waiter who happened to be nearby.

"She wanted to sit there," Bill said, eyeing Max anxiously. "I tried to give her another table, but she said it looked like it was the best table in the place. Secluded corner, great view of the ocean—"

"It *is* the best table in the place. That's why it's *my* table."

"Yeah, I know. I'm sorry about this, Max, but you've never come down this early before. And I didn't think it would do any harm. I figured she'd be long gone before you were ready to eat. Besides, it was a little hard to refuse her. Have you taken a good look at her?"

Max squeezed the bridge of his nose with his thumb and finger. "Yeah, I have. Never mind. Don't worry about it. She's bound to finish soon. I'll go check and see how close to being through she is."

Ashley swallowed the last of the scrambled eggs and reached for the big glass of orange juice just as Max walked up. "Oh, hi. I didn't expect to see you . . ." She wasn't certain how she should finish the sentence. She hadn't expected to see him—so soon? Today? Ever again outside her dreams? Maybe she should just be done with it and say not in this millennium.

Not that she was entirely unhappy that he was here now.

He dropped down in the chair across from her. "It would be difficult not to see me. You're staying at my inn. You also happen to be sitting at my table."

It wasn't peaceful when he was around, she decided. Just the sight of him kicked her heart into overdrive. He was too virile, too magnetic, too darned attractive, for her to ever find peace around him. And this particular moment in time was an excellent example of her problem.

His light brown hair was damp. He had probably just come from a shower, she decided, and wondered if other parts of him were still damp as well.

She was shocked at her thoughts, but she couldn't keep from continuing her survey of him. He had paired tan slacks with a short-sleeved knit polo shirt the same color of blue as his eyes. Hard, firm muscles showed on his upper arms, and to top everything off, he sat there so darned self-assured and relaxed, as if he was totally unaware of his effect on her.

"I'll move to another table," she said.

He waved his hand through the air. "That's not necessary. You look as if you're about through eating."

"Not really," she said, and glanced over his shoulder to see Bill approaching with a tray. "Scrambled eggs and bacon was just the first course. The second course is waffles topped with fresh sliced strawberries and whipped cream. Those *are* fresh sliced strawberries, aren't they, Bill?"

Bill grinned at her as he cleared her empty dishes and set the new ones in front of her. "They sure are."

"Good, because there's nothing worse than frozen strawberries on freshly made waffles. Don't you agree, Max?"

Max made no comment, but Bill beamed at her. "Will there be anything else?"

"No, thank you. Not right now."

"Max? Your usual?"

Max nodded, his gaze fixed firmly on Ashley. "You're going to eat all that?"

She smiled. "I sure am. This is the first meal I've had in days that wasn't served in Styrofoam containers."

"You didn't stop at any restaurants on your way here?"

She shook her head. "I got lost so often, and then once I found myself at certain places, like Graceland or Mount Rushmore, I wanted to see them, of course, so I tried to make up time by going to fast-food places. It didn't help."

She had the ability to completely absorb him, Max thought as he watched her eat. It was alarming how she made him forget things, like his boat down at the marina, like his impending trip, like his own breakfast. In fact, he was so absorbed in her that Bill startled him when he returned with Max's coffee and whole-wheat toast. He willed his nerves to quiet and stared at her, hoping it might make her eat faster.

Cutting herself another healthy portion of waffles and strawberries, Ashley glanced at the toast. "That's all you're having?"

"Yes."

"Would you like some of this?" She indicated the food on her plate.

"No, thank you. And if you keep eating like you are, you won't be able to get into those perfectly fitting designer jeans of yours by tomorrow."

He had noticed the fit of her jeans, she thought, pleased in a purely female, ego-satisfying way. Could it be possible that he was as affected by her as she was by him? In one way, it would be nice to know that she wasn't the only one who was feeling and thinking these things. But in another way, it could be disastrous.

His gaze dropped to the jade-green T-shirt she wore. CALGARY, CANADA was written across its front in script. The full, round shape of her breasts gave the words an enticing shape.

He took several deep swallows of his coffee and decided that, while he was waiting, he might as well make an effort at small talk. Besides, he was curious. "How do you know Ginnie?"

"Her husband knows my father through business. Ginnie and I met at one of those interminably dull dinners business people feel compelled to throw from time to time, and we've been friends ever since. When I mentioned to her that I wanted to get away for a while, she told me about your inn. You're really lucky to own such a great place."

"Thank you. What was it that you wanted to get away from?"

His question caught her with the fork in her mouth. She slowly pulled out the fork and chewed, giving herself plenty of time to think before she answered. "I didn't want to get away from anything exactly. Or for that matter, anyone. Not really. Well, maybe just a little. Well, okay, a lot, but basically I'm viewing this trip as a vacation. Everyone needs a vacation now and then, don't you agree?" Her answer sounded confused even to herself. As always, she should have taken *more* time to think, she mused ruefully.

"You have whipped cream on your mouth."

He was frowning at her, she noticed. "What?"

He leaned forward, staring intently at her mouth. "You have whipped cream right"—he extended his hand toward her, then quickly drew it back—"on your mouth."

"Oh." She patted the area with her napkin. "So how do you know Ginnie and Damien?"

"Damien has been my best friend for years. We went to business school together. He came out here a couple of years ago and met Ginnie. It was love at first sight."

"I'm glad for them, because they're really happy, and now they're going to have a baby, which is lovely. But in general, I don't believe in love at first sight. Do you?"

He wasn't sure. Talking to her, looking at her—hell, just being near her—made it hard for him to think straight. *She* was beginning to make sense. He regarded it as a danger sign.

"Your father wouldn't by any chance be Emmet Whitfield of Freeman and Whitfield, would he?"

Ashley's eyes widened with surprise. "Yes, he would. Do you know him?"

He nodded. "I know him in the same way that Damien does, as a business acquaintance. Before I retired, I worked on Wall Street."

"Really?" She wondered if he had met Roger, not that it mattered. "If you had stayed in New York, we would probably have met there instead of here. Amazing when you think about it. If you think about it, that is . . ." His eyes seemed to have turned a deeper blue, like the color of a glacier lake or a fine sapphire. But then, she supposed it could be a reflection of the light. Light had a way of playing tricks, she thought. Just like people had a way of playing tricks on themselves. "You're very young to be retired."

"By most people's standards, I am. But then, I've never much cared about other people's standards. And I happen to think that all that matters is that

I'm doing what I want with my life, and I'm not hurting anyone in the process."

"That's the real problem, isn't it?" she asked softly.

"What?"

"To do what you want without hurting anyone."

She suddenly sounded sad, he realized, and he found it curiously hard to tolerate. "What's the matter, Ashley?"

She tossed her head, sending her hair flying in a flaming arc behind her shoulders. "Nothing. Has the geranium been repotted?"

"The geranium? I haven't the faintest idea."

"I'll check at the front desk when I finish breakfast. And please remember to bill me for the post. I don't know what happened last night. I was tired and so happy I had finally gotten here, and suddenly there was the post and the geranium in front of me, and—"

"What did I say to make you sad, Ashley?"

"I'm not sad. Whatever gave you that idea?" She picked up a slice of strawberry and stared at it. "No, I just really admire the fact that you've carved yourself your own special place in life and that you're happy and at peace with that place."

"You're not happy and at peace?"

She popped the strawberry into her mouth. "Most of the time I'm very happy. And peace, well, sometimes that takes a little longer to find. Don't you agree?"

Gut instinct told him it would be folly to agree with her about anything. Just as continuing this conversation would be. "Where do those shadows in your eyes come from?"

"What shadows?" She didn't think anyone had

ever looked as closely at her eyes as he had; receiving the full concentration of his attention was beginning to make her uneasy.

He sighed. "Why did you come here, Ashley?"

"For a vacation. I thought I told you."

"What do you do when you're not on vacation?"

She felt as if she were being grilled. Not that she had anything to hide. She paused for a moment to review her last thought. No, she really didn't have anything to hide.

"You know, I hope you don't mind me saying this, but for someone who's retired and lives in this great place, you seem somewhat . . . tightly wound."

"Trust me. This time yesterday, I was extremely laid-back. Now answer my question. What do you do when you're not on vacation?"

She shrugged. "A little of this. A little of that. Anything that interests me."

"I'm surprised you didn't go to work in your father's brokerage firm."

"Oh, I did. But one day I hit a button on one of the computers and wiped out a whole day's sales."

He paled and sat back in his chair. "You hit *one* button."

"Well, I couldn't remember at the time what other buttons I had hit before I hit that one button. There's really no telling. Computers are such alien beings, don't you agree? I mean, doesn't it seem odd to you that a circuit board could hold information? Have you ever *seen* a circuit board? Totally unimpressive. So you have to ask yourself, *where* exactly *is* that information? I have my own theory. You know all those UFO spottings? Well, you never know who or what they've left behind. I think the Air Force should look into it and start their investigation with circuit boards."

He couldn't get past her hitting one button on the computer and wiping out a day's sales. Even though he had been retired from the business for several years, he was horrified by the thought. "It must have cost the firm millions."

"Yeah, more or less."

He stared at the smile that played around her mouth, thinking that either she was deeply disturbed or else he was. Then he saw the twinkle in her eyes. "You didn't do it, did you?"

Her smile broadened. "No. But I did work there for a while. It just wasn't for me."

The idea that she had been teasing him—and that he had bought it, hook, line, and sinker—had thrown him completely off balance, but he felt himself smile.

Her breath caught in her throat. "That's the first time you've smiled at me."

"I'm sorry. I don't know what's wrong with me." His smile faded, because he *did* know. Without any real, concrete reason he felt under seige. What's more, he noticed that there was still a smidgen of whipped cream on her upper lip. If he didn't get away from her immediately, he was going to kiss it off. He pushed back his chair and stood. "Enjoy your vacation, Ashley. I may not see you again. I'm planning a little trip."

"Oh?" Feeling a pang near her heart, she stood also. "When are you leaving?"

"First thing tomorrow morning."

She felt as if she had gotten lost again. Strange. "Well, have a good time."

"*Dammit.*" He snatched up his napkin and reached out to wipe her mouth. "You didn't get all the whipped cream," he muttered huskily.

She'd never find peace at this rate, she thought with despair, trying to deal with the way his body heat seemed to be wrapping around her. Maybe it was a lucky thing he was leaving. Yes, it was definitely lucky.

Ashley read the brass name tag of the pleasant-looking, middle-aged lady behind the front desk, then addressed her. "Hi, Marge, I'm Ashley Whitfield, and I'm a guest here at the inn. Do you happen to know if the geranium that was out front in a pot, but that's not out front in a pot anymore, has been repotted?"

Marge smiled and pointed behind her to a forlorn-looking plant sitting in a brass wastebasket. "It was there when I came on duty this morning."

"Cameron must have put it there," Ashley said thoughtfully. "Well, do you know if anyone plans to repot it? Cameron said the gardener would."

"I'm sure he will as soon as he gets to it."

Ashley shook her head. "I feel so responsible. I think I'll go into town this morning and see if I can find a new pot for it."

"Oh, that's not necessary."

"I know, but I'm feeling kind of restless. I think getting out of here for a while might help. Maybe it has something to do with the fact that this is the first time in days I haven't been behind the wheel of my car, and I miss it." She wasn't sure she believed that particular explanation for her restlessness, but fortunately Marge did.

"In that case, there's a nursery out on the highway. You can't miss it—"

"That's a very nice thought, Marge, but I wouldn't bet any money on it if I were you. I wonder, would it be too much trouble for you to draw me a map and explain the directions to me very carefully?"

Marge's pleasant expression never slipped. "I'd be happy to."

"Miss Whitfield!" Marge's eyes were round with astonishment as Ashley walked in the front door, a terra cotta pot under one arm, a bag of potting soil under the other. "You left six hours ago! Have you been in town all this time?"

Ashley nodded. "I think so. At any rate, I was in *a* town. But I did manage to get what I went after." She turned to a hovering bellboy and handed him her purchases along with a five-dollar bill. "If you could take these to the gardener, along with that plant behind the desk, I will be your friend for life. Oh, and one more thing. There are also a few bags of peat moss, potash, and phosphorous in my car. I don't like the look of the rhododendrons out front. Take everything to the gardener and tell him what I said. If he has any questions, have him give me a call."

"Sure will," he said with a grin, and rushed off to do her bidding.

"Are you a gardener?" Marge asked.

"I'm strictly an amateur, but I've always had an incredible green thumb. And if the plant doesn't get repotted by tomorrow, I'll do it."

"Don't worry. I'll see that it gets done myself." She glanced at her watch. "I go off duty at four, but I'll still have time to check on it."

"Thank you. I really appreciate it." She hesitated, then forced herself to look at the teakwood letter boxes on the wall behind the desk. "I don't have any messages, do I?"

Marge glanced over her shoulder, then back at her. "No."

"Good. That's very good." She hesitated again. "Uh, Max Hayden isn't around, is he?"

"No, I haven't seen him since this morning."

"That's good too. See you later."

She made her way across the lobby toward the back of the inn. Tall, wide mullioned windows brought the California sunshine into the large, open area. Pastel chintz couches and chairs created homey places for visiting and resting.

Max's inn was comfortable. *He* wasn't. To her, he seemed like a lighted stick of dynamite, although she wasn't entirely certain why.

Max was no doubt a very nice man once a person got to know him. And she was sure he would make a wonderful friend, not that she could ever see being friends with him. She reacted to him in the wildest way, almost as if she were falling in love with him. The idea was ridiculous, of course. Falling in love would lead to all sorts of things she wasn't ready for, things she would never in a million years be able to handle.

Coming to a stop at one of the windows, she stared out at the golden beach where people were sunning themselves and the blue-gray ocean that stretched to the horizon. Afternoon snacks and drinks were being served out on the terrace.

*She felt lost again.* Even when she had been wandering around today out on the highway, looking for a nursery, she hadn't felt this lost.

Normally being lost didn't bother her. A bad sense of direction was as much a part of her as her red hair, and she had always accepted both. But this particular lost feeling bothered her a lot, and strangely, it was the same kind of lost she had felt this morning when Max had told her he was leaving on a trip.

She needed to do something, she decided, like go for a walk on the beach, or maybe take a swim. But first she needed some California clothes. She turned and headed for the inn's boutique.

A short time later she had several bathing suits, summer outfits, and a T-shirt that said CALIFORNIA in her arms.

"Now tell me one more time where the dressing room is?" she asked the helpful clerk.

"Go out the door, turn left into the hall, and it's the fourth door on the left."

She smiled her appreciation. "Thank you."

She found the hall with no problem, counted four doors, and walked into a room darkened by drawn curtains. She fumbled for the light switch, flipped it on, looked around, and blinked. The room was equipped with a large teak desk, three computers, two printers, a fax machine, and two telephones. There was also a sofa and chairs, plus a large mirror on one wall. It was a little peculiar to have a desk in a dressing room, she mused, but it must be used as a multipurpose area.

After kicking off her shoes, she peeled out of her jeans and tugged on the bottom of a bright red bikini. It fit fine, she decided, and pulled off her CALGARY, CANADA T-shirt and bra. She was reaching for the bikini top just as the door opened behind her.

She threw a quick, panicked look over her shoulder, saw Max, grabbed the bikini top, and clutched it to her. "What are you doing in here?"

"I was just about to ask you the same thing." His gaze glued to her long-legged, almost bare form, he strolled in and shut the door.

"*I'm* trying on clothes."

"In my office, Ashley?"

She hastily crossed her hands over her breasts, holding the skimpy cups of the top to her. "The clerk told me this was a dressing room."

Fighting against the heating of his body, he walked slowly around the desk until he was facing her. "Somehow I doubt that."

"I'm telling you, she told me this was the dressing room."

"Why don't you tell me exactly what she said."

"She said to go down the hall, and the dressing room was the fourth door on the left."

"This is the fourth door on your *right*, Ashley."

She briefly closed her eyes. "Look, what difference does it make now? Just leave until I can get my clothes back on."

At the moment he didn't think a bomb explosion could make him leave. He shook his head. "I'm expecting an important call. It's why I came in here." He glanced over at the pile of things she had brought from the boutique. "A California T-shirt?"

"It's the only state I've been to that I didn't have a T-shirt from," she snapped. "Just step outside into the hall. I'll be as quick as I can, and then I'll leave, and you can have your office all to yourself."

He wondered if she knew how delectable she looked, half-naked, her hair in wildly disordered waves around her head. "You go right ahead with what you were doing," he said softly. "Don't let me stop you."

He had her caught. What's more, her heart was racing just as it had this morning when he had awakened and found her on his bed. She blew a strand of hair out of her eyes. "You know, not twenty minutes ago I was thinking that you were probably a very nice man once a person got to know you, but now I'm not so sure. You know perfectly well I can't tie or hook this top without exposing my . . . well, you know. . . ."

Holding her gaze, he circled the desk once again and stopped in front of her. "Tell me something, Ashley." His throat was tight, making his words sound rough. "Why is it that I can't seem to get away from you?"

"Well, I—"

He took her by the shoulders and turned her around so that her back was to him. "You take over my table, you invade my office—"

"Invade? Excuse me?"

"I'm not even safe from you in my own bedroom."

He had her there. Still, she crooked her neck so that she could glare at him. "You make me sound like some sort of contagious, incurable disease."

"It's a distinct possibility that I don't think I can afford to overlook." He gently pushed her head forward and gathered the length of her hair in his hand. A light, sweet scent assaulted him; the smooth, bare line of her back tempted him. Hunger rose swiftly in him. He gritted his teeth and somehow managed to hold on to his control. He thrust her silky wine-red hair over her shoulder. Then swiftly, adeptly, he tied the strings of the bikini top into a bow and hooked the clasp.

As quick as he had been, the touch of his fingers on her skin had sent heat skimming across her nerves. With the top safely in place, she slowly turned around. "Thank you."

Lord, she felt *bare*. She linked her hands together and told herself that she wouldn't feel self-conscious in the bikini if they were out on the beach. Just because they were in a room that seemed to be getting smaller by the minute didn't mean she should let herself fall apart. "You obviously know a lot about women's clothes."

He leaned back against the desk and regarded her solemnly. "I know enough, though normally I undress a woman before I dress her again. But then, you go against the norm, don't you?"

Flames burned in the depths of his blue eyes, flames she hadn't seen in his eyes before, flames she felt in her stomach and her thighs. "I-I'll just get my things and go."

"You can't leave here wearing that, Ashley."

"What?"

He hesitated and took a deep breath, trying to rein himself in before something happened that he would regret. "The top is too small."

She glanced down and saw that the red top only half concealed her nipples. Her hands jerked up, intending to cover herself, but he was quicker, running his finger along the top edge of one cup and one nipple.

She gasped as the flames inside her flared, stealing her breath and paralyzing her.

"The view is enjoyable to me," he said, his voice low and thick, "but I don't think I would like it if anyone else saw it."

Suddenly he bent his head and lightly pressed his lips to hers. Shimmeringly sweet sensations broke over her and through her, and she wasn't prepared when, all too soon, he jerked his head back.

Several seconds passed before she could propel herself into action and reach for her T-shirt. "I guess you're right. My parading through the lobby like this would be bad for business."

"That wasn't what I meant," he said gruffly.

Wondering what he *had* meant, she slipped the T-shirt over her head and pulled it down. "I'll take the top off in my room and return it to the boutique for the right size. It's nice these days the way you can buy one size bottom and another size top. It's helpful when you're bigger on top than you are . . ." She cleared her throat.

He drew her hair from beneath the T-shirt and arranged it around her shoulders as carefully and as artfully as if it were a silk shawl.

She fell quiet and let his fingers comb through her hair. Because she couldn't seem to think of anything else to do. Because she didn't want to move. Because she liked his touch.

"You're a definite problem, Ashley."

She didn't disagree with his judgment. "You could leave on your trip early."

"Yes, I guess I could."

"Or I could pay Cameron to drive me to another hotel."

"That would work too." He stared down at her for a moment, taking in the delicacy of her features, the fullness of her lips, the rapid rise and fall of her breasts. She was as affected by him as he was by her. And he was a heartbeat away from pulling her down to the floor and taking her.

But those damned invisible strings of hers . . .

"*No.*" He dropped his hands from her and put much needed distance between them. "There's no need for us to do either of those things," he said, once he was safely several feet away from her. "I'll keep my door shut tonight, and I'll answer my phone, and in the morning I'll leave."

She nodded, feeling oddly miserable and achy. "I'll eat at another table tonight."

"Good," he said in a strong and relieved tone, as if he had just made a difficult and momentous decision.


After getting the correct-size top and making the rest of her purchases, Ashley checked to see if any messages had come in for her. Relieved that none had, she had dinner in her room. Since Max had said he would keep the doors to his room shut, she felt safe in leaving hers open. She pulled a chair up to the French doors and sat, listening to the ocean's music and letting the gentle night breeze soothe her nerves.

But it didn't work. As the hour grew later, her agitation increased. An intended long, hot bath lasted five minutes. A book she had bought in the gift boutique failed to hold her attention.

She noticed that one of her nails was chipped, so she set about giving herself a manicure. She ended up smudging the polish and having to remove it.

It was around eleven-thirty when she heard the door to Max's room open and shut. Her heart leaped into her throat. He was there, just yards away from her. The thought sent her pacing and cursing. She was *never* going to get any sleep this way.

A sudden idea stopped her in the middle of the room. The inn had a steam room. It might help her nerves to relax and her mind to unwind.

She changed into one of her new bikinis, covered it with a short terry-cloth kimono, and as quietly as possible left her room.

With determination and concentration she managed to find the steam room, making only two minor wrong turns in the process. She was pleased with both herself and the fact that, due to the late hour, she had the place all to herself. This was going to work.

She kicked off her shoes, hung her robe on a hook, and entered the steam room.

Thick clouds of hot steam closed around her, and immediately she felt the tension begin to ease from her muscles. Moving blindly through the dense mist, she bumped up against the wooden bench and sat down.

On a man's lap.

# Three

Shocked and slightly off balance, Ashley flung out her hands. One came down flat on the man's chest, the other on his hard thigh. She immediately leaped up.

A dry, almost accepting voice came to her through the steam. "Let me guess. Ashley."

"*Max?*" She fanned the steam in front of her, trying to see him. "What are you doing here? I heard you go to your room just a little while ago."

"I was leaving my room. To come here."

"Oh."

"I guess I should have expected you. It's been over eight hours since our last encounter. I was due." He reached out his hand and encountered her bare midriff, then slid it up until he reached the edge of the bathing-suit top. "You bought the bikini."

"Yes, ah, I did. This one along with several others." His hand was lingering beneath her breasts, idly stroking her skin, as if he weren't aware of what he was doing. But she was. "Look, I didn't mean to barge in on you. I'll leave—"

"Wait!"

"What is it?"

He had tried, he thought. A battle had been waging in his head from the moment he had set eyes on her. He had never been the kind of man to take what he wanted without consideration, but his domination over the situation was rapidly disintegrating.

He circled her wrist with his fingers and gently pulled her down as he sat up. "Leaving won't solve a damn thing. We've tried that, and it doesn't work. Besides, there's plenty of steam in here for both of us. And even if there weren't, we seem to generate our own."

Heat twisted around her and in her, resurrecting her tension. "It would seem to me, just off the top of my head, so to speak, that the steam we generate between us would be enough reason for me to leave, don't you agree?"

His hand lightly skimmed over one of the cups that covered her breast, testing with his fingers the dimensions of what it shielded. "You exchanged it. This one's bigger."

"Yes. You're, uh, very good where women's clothes are concerned, but I said that before, didn't I?" She tried to scoot away from him, but his fingers hooked her swimsuit top and held her where she was.

"You know, Ashley"—his voice was low, raspy— "I'm beginning to think I really have no choice when it comes to you."

The backs of his fingers were pressing into the

soft flesh of her breasts. "Everyone has a choice, Max." Had he heard her? She had spoken barely above a whisper, but she didn't seem to have enough air in her to make her voice stronger.

"No, you're wrong. At least where you and I are concerned." His fingers delved inside the top, finding and stroking her nipple. "You've left me no choice whatsoever."

Heat was congesting in her chest; her limbs had lost all their strength. "Max—"

He reached behind her, and as if by magic, the top slid away. Then he took her breast in his hand. Knowing she should protest, knowing she should get up and walk out, she swayed toward him.

"You see, Ashley," he said thickly, "I've been going about this all wrong. I've been trying to *resist* you."

"You've been doing very well—"

"It's been hell, and I've just figured out what to do about it."

She knew before she asked. "What?"

"We're going to give in to what's between us, Ashley."

"No . . ." She put her palms flat against his chest, intending to shove away from him, but instead she found her fingers running through the dampened whorls of his hair and leaning her body into him, into the feeling.

"We both want it. You know it. I know it." He was pushing her, he thought, feeling a kind of pain he couldn't remember feeling before. It wasn't like him to push a woman or feel pain, but try as he might, he couldn't seem to stop himself. "Besides, it's the only way. You'll see. If we make love tonight,

I'll be able to leave in the morning without wanting you. It will work. It's *got* to." He bent his head, took her nipple into his mouth, and sucked.

Her body jerked. With a moan she burrowed her fingers in his hair and held his head to her breast. She was sure he could hear the heavy beating of her heart and feel her burning as with a fever. But there was something he didn't know, and she needed to tell him. . . .

"Th-There's something . . ." Lord, where had these sensations come from? Sensations that were like fire, that softened everything about her, making her pliable and amazingly willing. "Max . . . I need to warn you . . ."

He chuckled huskily and lifted his head. "Honey, you have warning signs posted all over you, but I've decided I can take the risk tonight as long as I leave tomorrow."

His finger flicked back and forth over her nipple as he spoke. The steam was opening up her pores; *he* was opening up her senses. Her concentration was slipping away. "Your plans sound—ahhh, maybe you shouldn't do that."

"What? You mean this?"

He rolled her nipple between his thumb and forefinger, sending fire streaking through her lower body.

"Yes, ohhh." She was just about lost, but she felt a moral obligation to tell him. She tried again. "Max, I'm not very good at sex."

"You're not a virgin, are you?" His tone held only mild curiosity.

"No." Her voice caught in her throat. "Well, I suppose not technically, anyway."

"Technically?" He transferred his attention to her mouth, stroking the pad of his thumb against her lower lip.

"I-I tried sex twice, but . . . I just never got the hang of it. It wasn't any good."

He skimmed his tongue along her lips, learning their texture and shape. "You know what you're doing, don't you?" he murmured. "You're giving me a challenge, and it's like throwing gasoline on an already raging fire."

The steam was wrapping around them, sealing them together in its soft, cottony heat. They needed to get out of here, she thought vaguely. They needed a cold blast of air. Something.

She moaned, because she didn't ever want to leave. And because she didn't know what to say to him. He thought she had challenged him, when she had only confessed. "Okay, then"—she took a deep breath, inhaling heat and his scent—"I made it to the state finals of sex three times and the nationals twice, but—"

He chuckled. "You're a terrible liar."

"Give me a little time. I'll get better."

"Your time has just run out, Ashley. Open your mouth."

What could she do to make him understand? He was right about her wanting him. But she knew what would happen if they had sex.

"Open your mouth, Ashley."

"It—it's open."

"Wider." He plunged his tongue deep into her mouth. He had already learned her scent, her feel, and, earlier today, he had had a brief taste of her. Now he took his time, learning the inside of her mouth and filling himself with her sweet, intoxicating, addictive flavor. And he still wanted more.

She wrapped her arms around him and let her fingers play over the slick, damp, hot skin of his back. The pleasure she was feeling was new and overwhelming, as were the intense sensations that were assailing her. She pressed closer to him, savoring the tight, exquisitely painful feel of her breasts against his chest.

"We need to get out of here," he muttered.

She'd had the same thought moments before, but she couldn't stop the sound of disappointment that escaped from her.

"It's all right," he said soothingly. "We're just adjourning to my room."

He stood and drew her up with him. "My bikini top," she murmured dazedly.

"I've got it."

And then they were outside, where there was light and cool air. And she still wanted him. But . . . "This isn't going to work, Max. I'm not any good at it. I'll disappoint you—"

He gently pushed her back against the tile wall and kissed her again. His tongue felt as if it belonged in her mouth, she thought, her head whirling. And his hard arousal was thrusting against her lower body, creating a hollow, hurting, infinitely exciting feeling inside her. Wrapping her arms around his neck, she decided that he might be right. Maybe they didn't have a choice. As awful as she would be, at least they'd get each other out of their systems.

A rough, tearing sound welled up from his chest, and he wrenched away from her. "If we don't get to my room and quick, I'm going to end up taking you right here." He glanced down at her high, firm breasts with their rose-beige tips, pointed and tempting him beyond anything he had ever known. He groaned. "Did you wear anything else down here?"

She was beyond saying anything. She gestured toward the hook where her robe hung.

He grabbed it, helped her into it, pushed the bikini top into one of its pockets, then shrugged into his own robe.

He looked at her and felt himself begin to tremble. "If you've never gotten the hang of sex before, it's not your fault."

She was leaning back against the wall, relying on it to keep her upright. "How do you know?"

He took a step closer, and when he spoke, his voice sounded tortured. "Because, Ashley, desire is in your eyes, on your face, on your skin. I can almost *smell* your desire. If I touched you, I would feel it. You were made for a man to make love to, I knew that from the beginning. You were made for *me* to make love to."

For a moment she could do nothing but stare at him. He saw her differently from the way everyone else did, even she herself. But he was wrong, and no matter what conclusions she had already come to, for his sake she had to try one more time before they were both hurt and disappointed. Somehow she gathered her strength and straightened away from the wall. "This isn't going to work, Max."

"Yeah, so you've said. But tell me you don't want me. *Tell* me, Ashley."

Defeated, she closed her eyes. "I-I can't."

His lungs hurt as he drew in short, ragged breaths. "I'm going to come apart if I don't have you soon." He reached for her hand, but the feel of it—so small, so soft—took his control so perilously close to the breaking point that he quickly dropped it. "Let's go," he said roughly.

Ashley walked by his side as they made their way out and up the short flight of stairs to the lobby. She didn't look to see if Cameron was at the reception desk. She didn't care. She was aware only of Max. She didn't know much about passion, but at the moment, she felt as if she were swimming through heat. Going with Max might not be the smartest thing she had ever done, but it was probably the most urgent, the most earth-shattering.

They reached the elevator, and Max jabbed the button. The elevator doors swished open.

*"Ashley, darling!"*

She stepped into the elevator, but Max stayed where he was. She gazed blankly at him. He had a strange expression on his face, and his body had gone totally rigid. "What—"

"Ashley, darling. We're here!"

Still uncomprehending, she followed his gaze to the petite older woman who was hurrying across the lobby toward them. The woman wore an elegant size-four Adolfo suit, her brown hair short and lacquered into place, her skin creamed and seamless. She knew the woman extremely well. *"Mother!"*

"Darling!"

And then she was being enveloped in her mother's arms and the unmistakable scent of Estée Lauder.

"Mother, what are you doing here?"

Her mother drew back and smiled up at her. "Where else would I be, darling? You're here, you obviously need me, and so I came. We would have been here sooner, but there was a mix-up at the San Francisco airport concerning our limousine, and we were delayed."

"We?" She didn't like the sound of the *we*.

"Naturally Leona's here with me." She turned and beckoned to the woman who was talking to Cameron. "Leona, look who I've found."

Leona was an inch taller than her mother and one size larger. Reed-thin, she wore a smart Chanel suit. Though both women had flown the entire width of the country, their appearance was flawless. Ashley, on the other hand, knew she looked as if she had been in the tumble-dry cycle of a dryer all night.

"Leona," she said weakly, as she submitted herself to another hug. "What a surprise."

Leona, who had always viewed Ashley as the daughter she had never had, beamed. "We knew you'd be surprised. Darling, we're going to have so much fun!"

"Uh, doing what exactly?"

"Why, anything you want, naturally," her mother said. "Whatever it takes. We're here for you."

"Takes?"

"To get you over these little prewedding jitters you're having, of course, darling."

"Prewedding jitters?"

It was the first time Max had spoken, and all

three women jumped at the harsh, grating sound of his voice.

Her mother's smile faded as she finally noticed him. "I'm so sorry. I'm Miriam Whitfield, and this is my good friend Leona Freeman. And you are . . . ?"

He gave her hand a perfunctory shake. "Did you say prewedding jitters?"

"Why yes. Ashley is engaged to Leona's son, Roger. We're here to make the plans."

"I see." His blue eyes glittered like hard sapphires as he gazed at Ashley. "I didn't know."

"Max—"

"And you are?" Leona asked, repeating Miriam's question but more pointedly.

He tore his gaze away from Ashley. "Max Hayden. I own the inn."

"How nice," she said, taking in his robe with narrowing eyes. "And you and Ashley have been swimming or something?"

"Yes. Or something. If you ladies will excuse me, I have to go up to my room. I need a shower."

Miriam gave a gracious nod. "Certainly. By the way, I assume that the proper rooms will be made available to us?"

"Oh, they already have," Leona said, indicating Cameron, who had stayed discreetly behind the desk. "That nice young man has been good enough to give us exactly what we require."

"I thought the inn was full," Ashley said hopefully.

"You're in luck," Max said, his face like stone. "It's Sunday night, and most of our guests have already left. Now, if you'll excuse me . . ."

"Max—"

"Darling," her mother interrupted, catching her by the arm to detain her. "You can talk to your friend tomorrow—if there's time—but for now come up to our rooms and help us settle in. We have so much to talk about. Leona and I are just brimming with ideas for the wedding."

Ashley opened the French doors and walked out onto the darkened balcony. It had taken a while, but she had finally gotten her mother and Leona unpacked and convinced them that she would not talk about the wedding tonight and that they should go to bed.

*What was she going to do about her mother and Leona?* She had expected phone calls, but not their arrival in person. She sighed. She had left New York to avoid exactly what was about to occur, and now she didn't know how to stop it.

And what about Max? Her cheeks heated just thinking about what had almost happened between them. If her mother and Leona hadn't shown up, she would be in Max's bed now. And, heaven help her, she had wanted just that. Still wanted it, if she was honest.

She glanced toward his end of the balcony. All the lights were off, and his doors appeared tightly shut.

He was furious with her, and she didn't blame him. Things between them had got completely out of hand, and it was probably all her fault.

She shoved her hands into the pockets of her robe, and her fingers encountered the bikini top.

She pulled it out and looked at it. It had taken him approximately a half second to take it off her, and only a little longer to get her to a heightened state of arousal. Most of those aroused feelings still boiled inside her, and the aching in her body told her she would run to him if he walked out those doors right now and held out his arms to her.

The doors remained shut.

"It's for the best," she whispered to herself. "It really is for the best." She slowly turned, walked back into the room, and shut herself in.

At the other end of the balcony Max sat in the dark, staring at the doors and wondering how in the hell he was going to make it until dawn without tearing those damned doors off their hinges and going to her.

Ashley barely slept, keeping her ears tuned for the sound of Max's door opening. She heard nothing. At dawn's first light she showered and dressed, then made her way across the balcony to Max's room. The doors were shut and locked.

When a knock drew no response, she hurried down to the front desk, gripped by the fear that he had already left on his trip. "Good morning, Marge."

"Good morning."

"Do you know if Max has left for Cabo San Lucas yet?"

"I didn't know he was planning to go, but then that's nothing new. He's got a plane, two cars, and a boat, and he often takes off in one of them at a moment's notice."

Ashley slumped against the reception desk.

"I did see him this morning, though."

Ashley straightened. "You did?"

Marge chuckled. "He never gets up this early, but he was up this morning. He said he was going down to the marina to work on his boat."

"That's great." She started off, but then stopped and came back. "Where's the marina?"

Marge grinned. "I'll draw you a map."

Several minutes later, map in hand, Ashley headed for the front door. Unfortunately her mother and Leona, still operating on Eastern Standard Time, chose that particular time to cross the lobby.

"Oh, there you are, darling," her mother said, sounding relieved. "I called your room, but when you didn't answer, we decided you might be down here."

Ashley thrust the map behind her back and eyed the two women with mixed emotions. She loved her mother with all her heart, Leona too. They were both so dear to her, yet she fervently wished they were back in New York. "I see you're planning a game of tennis," she said, indicating with a wave of her hand their crisp white designer tennis outfits.

"We never miss our daily game if we can help it," Leona said with a little laugh. "You know how we love the game. Besides, exercise is so important."

Ashley nodded, but privately thought that she could exercise twenty-four hours a day and would still never be a size four, or even a six. Next to her mother and Leona, she had always felt like a clumsy Amazon, though not because of anything they had ever done. She had always known she was loved and cherished, even when she had flunked ballet class.

"Finding you down here is such good timing," her mother said. "We were just going in for breakfast, and now you can join us."

"I've already had breakfast." In truth, she hadn't even had her morning Coke. It wasn't like her to lie to her mother, but if she didn't get to talk to Max before he left, she would never forgive herself. Sometime in the night she had decided to explain to him about her and Roger.

"Then come sit with us while we eat," her mother urged. "We have so much to talk about."

"Yes, we do," she said, "but right now I have an important errand to run."

A frown puckered her mother's smooth brow. "Why don't you just send one of the bellboys out for whatever you need, darling? You know if you go out, you'll get lost."

"Actually I've learned my way around the town quite nicely." Another lie. Her sins were mounting, she thought guiltily.

"That's wonderful. I'm so proud of you."

"Are there any decent shops in town?" Leona asked.

"Oh, yes." She supposed there must be.

"Good. Maybe we'll do a little shopping later."

"Sounds like fun. You two enjoy your breakfast and your game, and I'll be back before you know it." She leaned down and kissed her mother's cheek. "See you in a little bit."

Having made her escape, Ashley headed for the marina and Max. To her amazement, she didn't get lost once, and a short time later she was walking down the pier toward the sleek white cruiser tied up at its end. The name *Serendipity* was painted on the boat's stern.

There was no sign of Max as she boarded the boat, but she heard the sounds of a pop tune coming from an opening in the deck. Her heart beat with trepidation as she followed the music. She didn't expect that coming here would change anything, but she very much wanted him to understand.

She stopped at the edge of the opening and gazed down. Max was there, bent over a large piece of machinery, wearing shorts and nothing else. His broad shoulders gleamed bronze in the morning sun, and his muscles rippled beneath the smooth, supple skin of his back as he moved.

The sight made her mouth go dry. Last night those same muscles had rippled beneath her hands, and his skin had been hot. . . .

"Max?" *Darn.* He'd never hear her if she didn't get that whispery desire out of her voice, she thought, vexed with herself. Determined to do better, she screamed, *"Max?"*

He started, dropped a wrench, and swore. With an extremely unpleasant expression on his face, he turned and looked up at her. "What are you doing here? Never mind, you don't have to answer that. What were you looking for this time? A ringing phone? A table with a view? Another dressing room?"

Oh, yes. He was definitely furious with her. "I owe you an explanation."

She was wearing one of the outfits he had seen

yesterday in the pile of clothes on his desk—a skimpy bandeau and shorts made out of a yellow-gold cotton sateen. Under the bright sunlight, the color made her skin appear to shimmer and seem more golden. His body tightened; his temper shortened. "You owe me nothing, Ashley."

"Would you please come up here? I'm getting a crick in my neck. Besides, I can barely hear you for that radio."

With coiled tension in every line of his body, he hit the button on the radio and climbed up to her. "Okay, Ashley, now I'm here, and just in case you didn't hear me the first time, I'll repeat myself. You owe me nothing. In fact, I owe you an apology. I should have listened to you when you said it wouldn't work." He brushed past her and descended through a door to a lower deck.

"I wish people weren't always so surprised when I'm right," she muttered, and turned to follow him.

She found herself in a comfortable salon, the couches and chairs done in colors of aqua and sand. But once again, he was nowhere in sight. "Max?"

"In here," he said, his tone gruff but resigned.

She walked in the direction of his voice and came to a small, well-equipped galley. He was leaning back against the counter, a coffee mug in his hand.

"Want any?" he asked, indicating a coffeepot.

The close quarters of the galley probably weren't the best place for this encounter, she thought ruefully. He was too bare, too obviously virile. He seemed larger than life to her, with his bronzed skin, his broad chest furred with temptingly soft hair, his flat, muscled stomach, his strong, rock-hard thighs. His masculinity filled every corner and nook of the small area, endangering the supply of oxygen.

For a moment she forgot why she had come to see him. All she could think about was that they had nearly become lovers. What if . . .?

"Ashley?"

His impatient tone snapped her out of her reverie. "Uh, yes. Do you have a Coke?" she asked, hoping that a shot of caffeine would help clear her mind.

He retrieved a Coke from a small refrigerator beneath the counter and handed it to her. "Coming here wasn't necessary, Ashley. All I ask is that you don't send me an invitation to the wedding."

"There's not going to be a wedding—that's what I wanted to tell you."

He gave her a measured look. "You mother and her friend seem to feel differently."

"I know they do." She paused to take a much-needed drink of Coke. "They've been looking forward to this wedding ever since Roger and I romped together in our playpens. You see, our fathers are partners—"

"I know. Freeman and Whitfield."

"Right. Our families are extremely close, and Roger and I have always been the best of friends."

"Your mother said you were *engaged* to him."

She held up her hand. "I'm coming to that part. Unfortunately neither Roger or I have ever fallen in love with anyone else—"

"Meaning you have with each other?"

"You're really not making this easy for me."

"Don't hold your breath waiting for an apology."

She exhaled. "Please, Max, just let me tell you this my way. No, Roger and I have never fallen in love, not exactly, that is."

"Not exactly?"

She fixed him with the full wattage of her green eyes. He gazed back at her with hooded, deeply blue eyes.

She took another sip and willed the caffeine to kick in. "Okay, I think I'd better start over. You see, the thing is, I've never been able to stick with anything for very long. Jobs. Men. Hobbies. You name it. I tend to get preoccupied and drift away." She shrugged. "I don't know why. I just drift. I don't mean to, but it happens every time."

"You obviously stayed still long enough for Roger to give you a ring."

She nodded. "Yes, well, I'm still not sure how that happened, but then I had been really busy with a new job as a travel consultant. Things were going extremely well, I thought. I had had only a few minor setbacks, like the couple who got really upset with me because they found the Colosseum where I told them the Eiffel Tower would be."

"Excuse me?"

"I inadvertently sent them to Rome instead of Paris."

He looked at her.

"That story's true. At any rate, one day I glanced down and I saw the ring on my finger, and it dawned on me what it meant."

He let out a graphic curse. "Ashley, that is the stupidest thing I've ever heard."

She glared at him. "Did I say it was smart. *No*, I don't believe I did."

He rubbed his forehead, wondering where the headache had come from.

"So, anyway, there I was engaged, and I realized I needed to do something. Roger is a wonderful man, and I love him as a friend, but I could never be married to him. I could never be married to *anyone*. I'd drive a husband crazy."

"That's the first thing you've said that makes sense," he said grimly. "By the way, are you anywhere close to getting to the end of this story?"

She flipped a handful of hair behind her shoulders. "You're beginning to make me mad, Max."

Lord, she was lovely, he thought with something like despair. Emotion had heightened her color and put light in her eyes. He rubbed his forehead and the pain there. "Go on."

"Okay, so I told Roger."

"Told him what?"

"I told him that I couldn't marry him, and I gave him his ring back."

"You did?" he asked, surprised.

"Yes, that's what I've been trying to tell you. I'm not engaged anymore."

"And Roger knows this?"

"Of course. And he accepted it. I told you, we're the best of friends. He was busy with several new accounts and what-have-you anyway, and he was just as happy not to have to take any time off—"

He gave a sound of disbelief. "You *can't* be serious."

"Max, it's the truth. You didn't see him in the lobby of your inn last night, did you? No, you didn't. You just saw our mothers. He's back in New York, doing what he loves best, working."

He plunked his mug down on the counter and stared at it while he sorted through her story, looking for the flaws. He knew he would find something—and he did. "Then *why* do your mother and Mrs. Freeman think you're still engaged and that there's going to be a wedding?"

"It's simple."

"If that's true, it will be a welcome change."

"Max—"

"Just tell me, Ashley."

"They want us to marry so much, they can't accept my decision. And I knew they'd have trouble with it, so once Roger and I had our talk, and we told each of the families, I left town. I thought that if I wasn't around for them to try to change my mind, they'd eventually have to realize the wedding just wasn't going to happen."

"Your plan doesn't seem to have worked."

She sighed. "I know."

His gaze turned thoughtful. "So do you have a new plan?"

"Not really. I don't want to hurt them, they're both so sweet and well meaning. I guess I'll just have to stick to my decision and hope that they eventually realize it won't be the end of the world if Roger and I don't marry. I mean, after all, they'll still have us both." Gazing up at him through her lashes, she gnawed on her bottom lip for a moment. She had told him everything she had come to say, but she didn't feel any better. The tension between them was as thick, solid, and potentially hazardous as an electrified wall. "So, anyway, that's what I wanted you to know. I'm not engaged, but—"

"But?"

"But I think it's probably a good thing that they arrived when they did. They kept us from making a huge mistake."

A muscle flexed in his jaw. "How do you figure that?"

"I'm just not cut out to have a serious kind of relationship with a man." The fact had never bothered her before, but now she felt bewilderingly sad. "Remember? I drift?"

"I don't believe I said anything about wanting a serious relationship. In fact, that's the last thing I want."

Still holding the Coke, she crossed her arms beneath her breasts, hugging herself. "Yeah, well, my two experiences with one-night stands weren't all that great either, so I don't know what that leaves."

Not much of anything, he thought, wondering why he wasn't happier about it. Her philosophy of life fit in perfectly with his. Stay free and unattached and do exactly what you want. The trouble was, what he wanted was to take her to bed and keep her there for about a week. But no matter what he wanted, there were still those damned strings of hers to contend with. "Were either of your one-night stands with Roger?"

"Of course not. He's my friend."

"Right," he muttered. "Okay, Ashley, you've said what you came to say, now I've got to get back to work. You can find your way out, can't you? Or do I need to draw you a map?" A look of pain flashed across her face, and he felt like biting his tongue off. "I'm sorry."

"It's all right. Really." She leaned forward and placed the Coke can on the counter. "I can find my way out." She started for the door, then stopped and looked back. "Have a great trip, Max."

"I'm not going." The words were as much a surprise to him as they were to her.

"You're not?"

"No. At least not right now. I'm having a problem with the engine." It was a problem he could fix in an hour.

"Oh." She shrugged and gazed uncertainly at him. "Well, then, I guess I'll be seeing you around the inn. I'll do my best not to get in your way."

"Wait."

"Yes?"

What was it he wanted to say to her? "Stick around if you want to. I'm about to take the boat out for a trial run."

Her pulse picked up a beat at the invitation, and it was with regret that she turned him down. She shook her head. "I get seasick."

"The ocean's calm today."

"I once got seasick in a rowboat on a pond in Connecticut."

He stared at her, wondering what in the hell he was doing. "I have seasick pills."

"I can't swim."

"I'm Red Cross—certified."

She had a brief and not very fierce struggle with herself. "As long as we're not gone too long, I guess it will be all right."

All right? He was beginning to wonder if anything would ever be right again. Or normal.

# Four

As *Serendipity* sliced neatly through the water, forging a path across the blue Pacific, Max fixed his gaze on the horizon and tried to keep it there. He should be heading back to the marina soon, he thought without changing his course. Taking the boat out hadn't been necessary for him to know what was wrong with the engine, and he had gone much farther than he had planned.

Oh, what the hell, he reflected grimly. He might as well admit it. He hadn't *had* a plan. His only thought had been to keep Ashley with him a little while longer.

If he could find a jury, he'd plead temporary insanity.

Once again, he turned and looked at her. She was stretched out on her stomach on a cushioned lounger. And the dark tint of his sunglasses did nothing to shade his eyes from the glorious sight that Ashley's long, lithe body made in that little nothing outfit she was wearing.

A golden sheen gilded her skin. The breeze blew through her hair, creating wine-red streamers, and flirted with the wide legs of her shorts, allowing him tantalizing glimpses of the lace edge of her panties.

Gold. Her panties were gold-colored. Had they been one of the panties he had picked up off the lobby floor that first night? One of the satiny pairs he had fingered and that had introduced him to her sensual scent?

His jaw tightened. His gaze followed the straight line of her spine down to the graceful indentation of her waist, and came to a stop on her softly rounded bottom.

All that skin, all those curves.

*Dammit, she was going to burn.*

Slowing the boat, he checked the area around him for traffic, then engaged the automatic pilot at a low speed so the boat would hold its heading against the current.

Tossing his sunglasses aside, he strode over to her. "Where's the suntan lotion I gave you?"

She lifted the bottle from beside the lounger, rolled over onto her side, and propped her head up with her arm. "Here it is. Do you want to use it?"

"No. I want *you* to use it. You've barely got on any clothes, and you're going to be beet red in another ten minutes."

"I *have* used the lotion, Max." His hard, muscled form was blocking the sun. She should feel cooler, but instead she was feeling a heat that had nothing to do with the weather. Instinctively she sought to protect herself. "You don't have a surplus of clothes on yourself. Maybe you should use some lotion. Or put on some clothes. Or something."

"I'm used to this West Coast sun. Besides, my skin is like leather."

"It didn't feel like leather to me," she muttered under her breath.

"What?"

"Nothing. I'll use more lotion." She had no desire to argue with him. She rolled over onto her back and began to rub the lotion on her.

Everything male in him responded to the sight of her lifting her legs one at a time and stroking the slick emollient over her smooth skin. The hair on the back of his neck prickled; his muscles tensed. In desperation he glanced around for something that would save him and saw a beach towel. He grabbed it and threw it over her.

"What are you doing?" she asked, astonished.

"The protection factor in that suntan lotion isn't strong enough for you."

She sat up, the towel falling to her waist. "Max, you're being silly. I haven't been lying out that long."

"Long enough. And now look what you're doing—your back is exposed." With an oath, he dropped down onto the lounger beside her, jerked up its end, gently pushed her back against it, then pulled the towel up beneath her chin.

She looked at him. "Happy?"

"Ecstatic." He eyed her critically. "How are you feeling?"

"Fine. I haven't gotten seasick at all. I can't figure out why I haven't though."

"It's the pill I gave you."

She shook her head. "I haven't taken it yet. I figured I'd wait until I got sick before I took it."

"Why?"

"Because that's what you do when you get sick. You take a pill."

Maybe it was the way the light was reflecting off the water, he thought, but her eyes were more vividly green and the golden stars in her eyes more pronounced than he had seen before.

"There must have been something weird about that pond in Connecticut," she said.

"Maybe it was something you ate that day."

"Maybe. Or maybe it was the water. Now that I think about it, the water was a funny color. It wasn't quite blue. On the other hand, you certainly couldn't call it gray . . . or green . . . or . . ."

He was so close, she thought. Her rapidly beating heart told her he was *too* close. His face was roughened by a beard, making him appear even more rugged than usual. And that wasn't all that was bothering her about him. The wind had made a devilish disorder of his hair, and the sun added another layer of bronze to his skin. "You look like a pirate," she murmured.

In spite of himself, his lips quirked. "There you go again, saying exactly what you're thinking."

"Don't you like being compared to a pirate? I've always considered pirates very dashing and romantic."

"You think I'm dashing and romantic?"

She laughed. "Shoot, you have it all over the pirates of old. You're more than dashing—you have this sort of lazy, and at the same time powerful, sexuality. Believe me, that's a dangerous combination. It hits a woman between the eyes and makes her dizzy. And as for romantic—" Suddenly she realized the trap she had laid for herself; at the exact same instant she noticed the way his eyes had darkened. "No, actually I wouldn't say that you're romantic at all. You're too, uh, too . . . well, I'm sure you know what I mean." She cleared her throat. "In fact, I've been meaning to tell you that I don't think you're peaceful either."

He could certainly agree with that, he thought grimly. At the moment, he was aware of every nerve in his body.

She chewed on her bottom lip. "I guess you'll want me to move to another room."

"That might be a good idea." His voice was strained and hoarse. "I'll check with whoever's on the desk when we get back and set it up." His gaze lowered. The towel he had placed over her had shifted down, exposing her cleavage. The sight of the luscious, rounded breasts created an added tension in him. He pulled the towel back up until it was at her neck. "You need to stay covered up."

Irritated both by his nearness and by the fact that he thought it was a good idea that she move out of the room that was next door to his, she jerked the towel back down. "I'm *not* going to burn."

"Yes, you will."

"No, I won't."

His teeth clenched with a snap. "Does the phrase 'boiled lobster' mean anything to you?"

She glared at him. "Yes, it's one of my favorite meals."

He grasped the edge of the towel and tugged it upward. She yanked the towel in the opposite direction. The towel tore. His fingers brushed against her breasts. She inhaled sharply.

The crackle of the ship-to-shore radio rent through the charged air.

"Ashley? Ashley, darling? Are you there? This is your mother. Over. Mr. Hayden, my daughter's there, isn't she? This is Miriam Whitfield, and I must speak to my daughter. Over."

"I think it's for you," Max muttered, surging to his feet with barely suppressed anger.

She grimaced, stood, and followed him toward the helm. She heard her mother say, "No one is answering, and I'm saying Over. Ashley? You're there, aren't you? I have the most fantastic news. BoBo Dupree has arrived, and she's brought the most divine surprise."

"What's a BoBo?" Max asked, his face dark, his eyes stormy.

"She's a wedding consultant."

"Wedding consultant?"

"You know, she helps plan and coordinate weddings."

A muscle moved in his jaw as he thrust the handset at her. "Push the button when you want to speak and say 'Over' when you're through. Tell your mother we're heading back right now."

"Ashley, you look beautiful tonight," Leona said. "I wish Roger were here to see you. Did you like your new clothes? Your mother and I did a little shopping before we left home. We thought perhaps a few new outfits would cheer you up."

"They were all very nice." She had found th "few" new outfits filling her closet when she had returned to her room, and she recognized the designers of each. Because she knew that ultimately she was going to have to disappoint Leona and her mother, she had decided to wear one of the outfits to please them. She had chosen a silk pants suit consisting of a draped purple bustier top and full-cut wine, purple, and fuchsia crepe pants.

Her mother leaned toward her. "Darling, while you were out on Mr. Hayden's boat—"

"That reminds me. How did you know where I was?"

Her mother shrugged. "The lady at the front desk was extremely helpful. She said that you had gone down to the marina to see Mr. Hayden about something, and she helped me place the call. I knew you would want to come back as soon as possible once you knew BoBo was here. I didn't actually know the boat had left the marina." She fingered the pearls at her neck. "I'm not sure it was entirely wise of you to go out with Mr. Hayden, considering your engagement."

"Please, Mother, no lectures. Besides, you know I'm no longer engaged," she added, although she realized the statement would fall on deaf ears. She scanned the dining room, searching for Max. She had taken great pains to tell the waiter which table she wanted so he wouldn't mistakenly place them at Max's table, thought he probably wouldn't come down for dinner. He'd seemed so angry with her on the trip back to the marina. But then again, she had managed to rub him the wrong way practically from the moment she'd arrived here. Except for those minutes they had spent together in the steam room . . .

"You know I wouldn't dream of lecturing you, darling. Anyway, you're going to be really interested in learning what I found out about Mr. Hayden."

Her attention snapped back to her mother. "Lord, Mother, you didn't have him investigated did you?" It wasn't something Ashley would put past her.

"Why would I do that? No, I simply asked a question here and there, plus I spoke with your father. Did you know that Mr. Hayden used to be a very big man on Wall Street, and that several years ago he gave it all up, bought this place, and retired?"

"He told me that he had worked on Wall Street."

In her excitement Miriam gave one of her infrequent unladylike snorts. "He did much more than merely *work* there, darling. He, along with Damien Averone, plus a handful of others, pretty much ruled supreme for quite a few years. I don't understand why we've never met him before."

"Maybe he didn't care for the social scene," Leona said. "A great many people don't, though I've never been able to understand that sort of thinking."

Miriam nodded in agreement. "Anyway, I feel better knowing his background. And, Ashley, I can now understand why you've made friends with him. You two have very similar backgrounds."

But she hadn't made friends with him, Ashley thought. And they had no relationship other than the fact that they seemed to bother each other a great deal.

Just then she saw him. He was standing in the doorway, exchanging a few words with the head-waiter, but his gaze was on her. She averted her eyes, but his image was seared into her mind. He was wearing a light blue sports shirt paired with navy-blue pants and sports jacket. He looked *great*. More than great, actually . . .

The conversation her mother and Leona were having was nothing more than low-pitched background noise to her. Once again Max seemed to be filling up her senses, interfering with not only her hearing but with her thought processes. Slowly she turned her head and looked back at the doorway.

*He wasn't there*, she realized with unreasonable panic. Her gaze flew around the room until she found him. He was sitting at the adjoining table, reading a newspaper. *His* table.

She had asked the waiter to place them at a table she had known would be next to his, and she hadn't realized it until that moment. The thought sent her mind spinning. Wonderful. On top of everything else her subconscious was playing tricks on her.

"Oh, good!" Leona said, her tone one of true delight. "BoBo's here!"

Ashley turned to see BoBo Dupree threading her way through the tables. A tall, matronly, perfectly turned-out woman, BoBo was dressed all in peach, from the bow in her hair to her tinted hose and matching shoes. For years BoBo had been New York society's premier wedding consultant and party planner. That she had an eccentricity made her all the more popular.

And, Ashley noted wryly, that eccentricity was following her through the crowd now. *Sybella*— the divine surprise her mother had spoken of on the ship-to-shore radio.

Sybella, BoBo's personal astrologer and spiritual adviser, was not only a woman with just one name, she was also a woman who had Brillo-pad hair, clothed her short, compact body in voluminous, robelike clothes, and literally dripped with crystals of all sorts.

Miriam graced each woman with a warm smile. "BoBo, Sybella, have a seat. We've held off ordering until you got here."

Elegant and perfumed, BoBo sank into a chair. "How kind of you. Sybella and I haven't had a thing to eat since we left New York. We both detest airline food. Ashley, how good to see you again."

"BoBo," she murmured with a nod. "Sybella." Sybella never spoke unless she was uttering pronouncements or ordering food. Currently her Brillo-pad head was buried in the menu.

"They have the most divine seafood here, ladies," Leona said. "Oh, good, here comes our waiter."

At the next table Max tried to concentrate on what he was reading, but the words kept blurring in front of his eyes. Ashley looked breathtaking in that outfit. Her bare shoulders gleamed, and her hair had been brushed to a lustrous shine. *Dammit.*

He had known she would be here. In fact, if he

was honest with himself, he would have to admit that she was the reason he had come down. He didn't know why, except that his muscles were coiled so tightly he was hurting, and he hadn't been able to stay away.

"Ashley," BoBo said, "I want to reassure you that your and Roger's wedding is going to be a *magnificent* affair!"

"I haven't been concerned—"

"Good, that's good, because none of us want you to be concerned." BoBo turned to the two mothers. "I must compliment you ladies on this idea. Having everyone fly out so we can plan the wedding here was nothing short of brilliant. Everything here is so cozy and relaxed, and we're really going to be able to get a great deal accomplished."

Ashley shot her mother and Leona a glance. "Actually, BoBo, perhaps you haven't heard, but Roger and I have called off the engagement."

A bright smile fixed on her face, Leona spoke up. "No, darling, *you* called off the engagement. Roger, poor dear, is back in New York, burying himself in his work, waiting for you to come to your senses."

Ashley rolled her eyes. "Please, Leona. Roger always buries himself in his work, and he's known for a long time that there's no hope for my senses." She shook her head. "The engagement is off, ladies, and therefore, extending the logic just a little bit further, I'm confident you will all see that the wedding is also off."

Miriam shook her head in distress. "Darling, I had no idea how *strong* these prewedding jitters of yours were. But don't worry about a thing. You're going to be a beautiful bride."

"Your mother's right, Ashley," BoBo said. "Believe me, in my business I've seen hundreds of cases of prewedding jitters, and I can tell you with great assurance that they always pass."

"But—"

Suddenly Sybella reached into the folds of her robe and brought out a laptop computer. She set it up on the table and began typing away.

BoBo smiled broadly. "Sybella feels that since the two lovebirds never got around to setting the wedding date, the problem must be that Ashley is concerned about the date. Sybella plans to come up with the exact date that will be astrologically correct and ensure the happy couple a long and prosperous marriage."

Leona clapped her hands together. "How wonderful."

Ashley's mind drifted to Max. He appeared to be absorbed in the business section of the newspaper. She remembered the computers and fax machine in his office. Obviously he still kept his hand in the business world. As she watched, he lifted his glass of wine and sipped. The strong column of his throat moved as he swallowed, and she had the funniest sensation that she could feel the warmth of the wine in her stomach.

". . . and the church will be flooded with sunlight, and there'll be banks and banks of white flowers, and—"

Ashley looked at BoBo. "How do you know the church will be flooded with sunlight? It might be raining that day."

BoBo beamed triumphantly. "Even if it is, we'll have spotlights set up outside, shining on the windows, to create the illusion of sunlight streaming in!"

Miriam made a sound of ecstasy. "BoBo, you are absolutely the best, bar none."

"I know."

Sybella's fingers continued to fly over the keyboard of her laptop, and Ashley hazarded another glance at Max. Her gaze collided with his, and she felt heat sear across her skin.

"We should look into renting the Waldorf for the reception," Leona said, "and I think it would be a nice touch if we had trumpeteers call the guests in to dinner."

"Good idea."

With a viciousness that told only part of his mood, Max sliced into the steak a waiter had just brought him. Dammit all to hell, Ashley was going to end up getting married, and she wasn't even going to *know* it until it was too late! Just exactly as she had gotten engaged.

She was sitting over there, appearing to listen to what they were saying, but he could tell she wasn't hearing them. Her mind was on something else, though heaven knew what. Abruptly he signaled the waiter for more wine. He had never in his life met a more frustrating woman!

She lived a free-form life, drifting from one thing to the next. And as far as he could tell, her only boundaries were those created by her wish not to hurt those she loved. Which was fine, except he was very much afraid she would end up married to a man she didn't love.

Her mother and her friends weren't listening to her when she told them she wasn't going to marry

Roger, and she wasn't listening to them while they went merrily on their way, planning the wedding. And from the sound of it, Roger would go along with anything as long as it didn't interfere too much with his work.

Somehow he had to make her understand that she was about to drift into the biggest mistake of her life.

With a grand flourish Sybella hit a key on her keyboard, much as a concert pianist might hit the final key of a Rachmaninoff concerto. "The third Saturday in September!"

BoBo grinned. Leona and Miriam gasped with admiration. Ashley looked as if her mind were elsewhere.

Muttering a string of oaths, Max pushed away from the table and stalked out of the dining room.

Ashley's heart sank as she watched Max leave. He was furious, and no doubt it was with her. She couldn't explain exactly why, but he had grown important to her. It was as if she could breathe more easily when she knew where he was and what he was doing. And she hated it when he was angry with her.

She wanted to go to him and try to make things all right between them. But that would be foolish, because he had made it clear he didn't want to have anything to do with her. As soon as she could politely excuse herself, she went to the front desk to see which room they had assigned her— and discovered that she was still on the third floor.

"Max did inquire," Cameron said, "but your mother has reserved a block of rooms for her guests and—"

"Excuse me," she said, "but did you say a *block* of rooms? A block as in a *whole bunch*?"

Cameron nodded. "That's right. She's expecting quite a few people over the next couple of days, and combined with our other reservations, there just aren't any rooms available."

"I see. And how did Max take this news?" Cameron bent his head and began sorting through reservation cards. She sighed. "He wasn't thrilled, was he?"

With obvious reluctance Cameron looked at her. "Well, not exactly. I was surprised. I thought he'd be glad that we're going to have another full house."

But he hadn't been, she thought miserably, because he wanted her off his floor and now she had to stay there. "Thanks, Cameron."

Up in her room she took a long, hot bath, trying to soak away her unhappiness. Max's displeasure with her was like a heavy weight on her heart.

But she couldn't just up and leave the inn and go some other place. She had already tried leaving her mother and Leona once, and the plan had been a dismal failure. This time she had to stay and make them realize she meant what she said.

The only other alternative would be to convince everyone to fly back to New York in the morning and go with them. The problem was, her mother, Leona, BoBo, and Sybella seemed extremely happy with their surroundings. Besides, her mother was expecting other people as well, though Lord knew who.

Dispirited, Ashley climbed out of the tub, dried off, and slipped a lightweight white cotton nightgown over her head. It had an embroidered bodice, delicate lace straps, and its short, ruffled hem billowed at her knees as she walked to the French doors to open them.

The moon was nearly full and had turned the beach a silver color. The ocean air played in her hair, and the sound of the crashing waves soothed and stirred. Just for a moment she was again gripped by the urge to see Max. She wanted to continue on down the balcony to his room and try to talk to him. Maybe they could work out a truce.

She exhaled a long breath. Whom was she kidding? For a truce to work, there needed to be a cessation of tension between the parties concerned. Unfortunately the tension between her and Max was a tangible, pulsing thing, and with so much substance, BoBo could have it decorated and use it as a theme for one of her parties.

Ashley chewed on her bottom lip, pondering her idea. It could be a combination Life-on-the-Fast Track/PMS party. As centerpieces BoBo could use attaché cases painted with dart targets on the sides and give out Midol and Alka-Seltzer samples to each guest.

Stupid idea, she thought with a grimace. Returning to the room, she turned out the lights and climbed into bed.

But she couldn't rest.

Her mind raced; her body ached. In the moonlight-spliced darkness, the memory of Max as he had been on the boat came back to her. He'd been very bare, very bronzed and muscled, in those shorts he had had on. His presence had filled up that small galley, and strangely she had felt as if he were filling her up too. Strangely because she really didn't know how it would feel to have him thrust into her and take full possession of her.

Frowning and restless, she slid her legs across the sheets. She had almost known what it would be like. *Almost.*

He had wanted her when they had been in the steam room. And heaven knew she had wanted him. Her breasts had swelled as they had pressed against his hard chest, and her lower body had hurt for him and felt achingly hollow. She remembered it all. . . .

A silhouette of a man appeared in the doorway.

"Max," she whispered, no doubt in her mind who it was. Who else could change the texture and temperature of the air until it was thick and hot?

He moved silently across the room to her. When he reached her side, he balanced a knee on the edge of the bed and stared down at her.

She returned the stare, struck by how magnificent he looked. He still had on the slacks he had worn earlier, but he had removed his shirt and jacket. And in the silver-tinted darkness, his eyes were dark . . . and burning.

"Max?"

Slowly, silently, inexorably, he lowered himself over her, then claimed her mouth with his.

The heat hit her so fast, she forgot her initial surprise at seeing him in her room. The weight of his body on hers was both new and thrilling. And when his tongue plunged into her mouth, she instinctively met it with her own. Their tongues tangled and danced together; he gave a rough sound of satisfaction and deepened the kiss.

Sparks of desire shot through her, stealing her will.

For once in her life she didn't try to talk. Telling him a relationship between the two of them would never work out was useless. How could she argue when wondrous feelings were wreaking sensual havoc on her body? A need was beginning to grow low in her belly, and she couldn't deny him.

His mouth sought out her throat and nibbled, finding places that turned her boneless. Then he rocked his pelvis against hers, and passion streaked through her, eliciting a moan from her. There was a strength about him that excited her, a male virility against which she had no defense.

Still silent, still in command, he rolled to one side and roughly pushed up the hem of her gown. Air flowed over her heated skin. Her nipples were already tight and throbbing, and when his tongue circled one and his mouth took sure possession, the need grew.

With a gasp she closed her hands in his hair. She could hear the sound of him quietly sucking at her breast, feel each tug as fire lanced through her belly. The pleasure was piercing and almost unbearable, but she wouldn't have given it up for the world. In fact, she wanted more. Her hips arched upward, seeking but not finding.

And the need grew even stronger.

She heard herself whimper, and when his fingers delved between her legs, she opened to him like a flower. Nothing was easier or simpler, or had ever felt as fantastic. No one had touched her as he was doing now. Nothing had ever felt or meant as much as this. She wanted to tell him how exquisite the pleasure was and how with each movement of his fingers she felt as if she might come apart. But she couldn't speak.

White-hot heat coursed through her like a river raging out of control. And suddenly the need couldn't be contained any longer.

"Max!" Blindly, compulsively, she reached for him.

But he wasn't there.

He was standing by the bed, his hands fisted at his side, his chest rising and falling.

"Max?"

"Do you want me to make love to you, Ashley?" he asked, the words rumbling up from his chest, harsh and raw.

"Yes." The pain in her voice vaguely surprised her.

"Good. I want you to remember how you feel right at this moment. Remember and don't forget. Then, on that day when you wake up and find yourself marching down the aisle, maybe you'll realize that marrying Roger would be a disaster."

Dazed, she lay there and watched him vanish out the door and into the moonlight.

# *Five*

Her whole body was pulsating and on fire for him. And he had walked out on her. What had happened? She pressed a hand to her head, willing her mind to clear.

*What* had he said? Something about her marrying Roger? None of it made any sense to her.

As she sat up in bed, her nightgown slid down to cover her, reminding her. Dammit, he came into her room, practically undressed her, *practically* made love to her, and then had *walked out*!

Anger began to replace the need. She slid off the bed and hurriedly put on the first thing she saw— the outfit she had worn that morning. She looked for her shoes, couldn't find them, and decided to forget them.

She marched down the balcony to his room. The doors were open, but he wasn't there.

She hurried downstairs to the lobby. "Cameron, have you seen Max?"

As always, Cameron was pleasant and eager to please, but there was also a certain wariness about him that told her she wasn't hiding her anger well. "The boss left a few minutes ago. Is there anything I can do for you?"

*"Left?"* No, no, no, she thought. Max wasn't going to sail merrily away while she was left here fuming about what had just happened. "The marina, right? He went to the marina."

"Uh . . . he didn't say a word to me."

"Never mind." She turned on her heels and headed for her car. Even though she had been to the marina only once before, she drove without fear of losing her way. She could get lost in her own apartment back in New York. But Max was like a lodestone to her. She never seemed to have any trouble finding him, no matter where he was. She could find him even when he didn't want her to, even when *she* didn't want to.

Once at the marina, she located the correct pier with no trouble. Down at its end she could see the running lights of his boat. The thought that he might be about to take off gave her an additional urgency and added to her fury. She ran the length of the pier and jumped onto the boat just as Max started its engine. She grabbed his arm before he could engage the gears and jerked him around.

His expression was harsh and reckless, but she wasn't deterred. "Just exactly what did you think you were doing back there in my room?" she yelled.

He was completely taken off guard by her sudden appearance. One second her image had been burning in his mind, the image of her quivering and willing beneath his hands. The next, she was standing in front of him, vibrating with anger, and more beautiful than he had ever seen her. But his anger matched hers, and he yelled back at her. "I was trying to show you what a gigantic mistake you're about to make!"

"*Mistake?* Oh, you mean the mistake I made by giving in to you as easily as I did. Now, *there's* a gigantic mistake for you, and one that I can assure you won't be repeated."

"Fine! Whatever you want! But just know that if you marry Roger, you'll regret it for the rest of your life."

Wind whipped her hair across her eyes. Impatiently she swiped it from her face. "Roger? You mean *he's* what all that was about? You came to my room because of *Roger*?"

"Dammit, Ashley, don't you *get* it? You can't respond to a man like you did to me and get married to someone else. And, baby, did you ever respond! I could have taken you right then and there."

Irate and embarrassed at hearing the truth, she felt her cheeks flush with color. "You give yourself *way* too much credit!"

"No way, lady. Ten more seconds, and I would have been inside you."

But he hadn't done it because he hadn't wanted her, she thought, growing even angrier. "You are the most egocentric, crude, unpleasant, uptight—"

"Don't leave out 'bastard.' What's got you so upset, Ashley? The fact that I didn't finish what I started?"

He caught her wrist in midair, stopping her

before she could hit him. She had never slapped a person in her life, and she was shaken by the idea that he had driven her to the point where she had tried. She wrenched her wrist from his grip and made an attempt to lower her voice. She was only partially successful. "Damn you, Max, haven't you been *listening* to me? I'm not marrying Roger."

"Yeah, I heard you, but the mothers of the prospective bride and groom didn't, and, dammit, Ashley, if you're not careful, you're going to wind up *married*."

She planted her hands on her hips and glared at him. "And so you thought you'd take it upon yourself to give me a little practical demonstration that would remind me why I shouldn't marry Roger. How very kind. Just who in the hell do you think you are, anyway? How *dare* you do something like that!"

He stepped closer to her, his eyes glittering with inner fire. "How dare I? I'll tell you how I dare. By your own admission, you didn't know you were engaged until one day you looked down and saw a damned ring on your finger."

The fact that it had happened just that way didn't lessen her anger by one iota. "I explained that! I was busy!"

"Right. You were busy. Your mind was on other things. Paris-Rome, Rome-Paris, I can understand. Those are two cities I often confuse because they're so much alike."

"It can happen," she said, furious.

"Obviously it can if *you're* making the reservations. You should come with a label; *Warning: Mind will change direction without notice.*"

"That's not funny!"

"Tell me about it. I watched you tonight, Ashley. I listened. Something sure as hell was on your mind other than what those women were saying. I give them forty-eight hours to have your whole damned wedding planned."

"You're exaggerating."

"Not in the least. If you heard two words they said, I'd be surprised. And call me simple, but I can't figure out what could be more important than convincing them that you're not going to marry Roger."

"I don't understand what your problem is, Max. Mother and Leona mean well, and they're eventually going to understand."

"How? When? You don't even pay attention to them long enough to comprehend what they're doing."

Her brow creased. "So what if I don't? I've known them all my life. I know how they think. They're not saying anything I haven't heard before. And what is it to you anyway? Why do you care?"

"Why? *Why?*" He looked at her in frustration. Her green eyes blazed; her skin was flushed and glowing; her hair flew wild and free around her. Her taste was still in his mouth, her feel still on his hands.

*He loved her.* The knowledge hit him like a sledgehammer between the eyes.

He had been right to fear her, but in the end he'd never had a chance.

She crossed her arms beneath her breasts. "Are you going to answer me, Max. Why?"

If he told her the truth, it would scare her to

death. She had already said she wasn't cut out to have a serious relationship with a man, and now he knew he wouldn't settle for anything less. "Because I hate witnessing accidents, and that's what a wedding between you and Roger would be—a terrible, catastrophic accident." He swung around and hit a switch to turn off the boat's engine. The sudden quiet was startling. "Unless," he said, lowering his voice, "you really do want to marry him."

She frowned, wondering why he was no longer yelling at her. "We've already been through that, Max. I told you I don't. And if you were paying as close attention as you say you were tonight, you would have heard me tell everyone the same thing."

"Yeah, and I also heard the impact it made. Nil."

The air was cool on her skin, but she was so engrossed with him, she scarcely felt it. Her system still had not recovered from his lovemaking. She wanted to hurt him as much as he had hurt her. "I can't believe you're actually standing there, critiquing my conduct at dinner tonight! If you have such an aversion to accidents, then I suggest you look the other way, *not* that one is about to happen, mind you. And anyway, as far as I can see, it's not any of your business."

He had made it his business even before he had realized he loved her. Now that he knew, there was no way he was going to let a wedding between her and Roger take place. "Maybe you're right, but satisfy my curiosity. What exactly was on your mind tonight?"

Emotions ran rampant through her, buffeting

her, repeatedly striking everywhere inside her that she hurt. She felt disoriented and wildly out of control. "*You*, dammit. I was thinking about you! How I irritate and bother you. How you want me to move off your floor. How you're always trying to get away from me, even though I'm not stalking you, except for tonight when I felt perfectly justified in . . ." Something about him was different, she realized. He no longer seemed harsh or reckless. There was a warmth in his eyes, a gentleness in his demeanor. "Max—"

His hands closed around her upper arms. "I'm sorry, Ashley."

His apology was so unexpected, her mouth fell open. "What?"

"I'm sorry for getting angry about the dinner this evening. And I'm sorry for coming to your room and going as far as I did, then abruptly leaving." He paused, and his voice turned husky when he continued. "And I guess the thing I'm the *most* sorry about is that I didn't make love to you."

Ashley stared at him, stunned. "You are?"

Although he still held her arms and could have effortlessly drawn her to him, he went to her, closing the small distance between them so that their bodies lightly touched. "I want very much to make up to you what I did. I want *you* very much—I can't even begin to tell you how much."

Where had her anger gone? she wondered, bewildered. How could he vanquish her righteous indignation so easily? "If that's the case, why did you leave like you did?"

"Looking back on it, I think it was the dumbest thing I've ever done in my life. It was also the hardest thing I've ever done, and believe me, I paid for it physically. I'm still paying for it. Every nerve, muscle, and bone in my body is hurting for you."

Slowly he lowered his head, giving her plenty of time to pull away. When she didn't, he lightly brushed his lips across hers. At the touch of his mouth heat began to thread through her.

"Forgive me, Ashley," he whispered. "Please forgive me."

"Don't do it again." It seemed important for her to say that. But she knew if he came to her again, brought her to the point where she would do anything he asked, and then left, she wouldn't be able to stop the pain from completely engulfing her.

"Never. I *couldn't*. Make love with me, Ashley."

The thread of heat became a stream growing wider, rushing faster. She started to remind him that she wasn't any good at sex, that they would both be disappointed, but desire stopped the words in her throat. For a brief period of time anger had obscured her need for him, the need he had created in her moonlit room. But the need had remained inside her, and now that she was no longer angry, it surged with full, thundering force. "All right."

A hard shudder raced through him. He touched the soft curve of her cheek, then took her hand and led her downstairs, through the salon, to a hall. At the end of the hall he opened a door.

She saw a blurred image of a luxuriously furnished bedroom and an oversized bed. Only Max was crystal-clear to her. A fiery passion showed in his brilliant blue eyes and on his taut face, but he was overwhelmingly tender as he reached behind her and unhooked the bandeau. It slid to the floor without a sound.

Holding her eyes, he undid his slacks, pushed them down past his hips to his knees, and then stepped out of them. His lips moved as he murmured to her, but her heart was hammering so hard, she couldn't hear.

His lips moved again. She concentrated on the words and heard, "Don't be afraid."

"I won't," she whispered, watching with mesmerizing wonder as his briefs came off.

She had thought she knew what a naked man looked like, but she had been wrong. Max was a marvel to her. He was all powerful muscles, smooth, glistening skin, and undeniable virility. To her own surprise, she reached out to him, wanting to explore him, and found herself delighted by the tiny nubs of his nipples beneath her fingertips.

The sound of his harsh, indrawn breath at her touch emboldened her. She skimmed the flat of her hand down his muscled abdomen to his navel, and then, after a moment's hesitation, lower to his hard arousal. Tentatively her hand closed around him. He made a rough, broken sound.

"Do you want me to stop?" she asked.

"Lord, no . . . *please*, no."

Lured and fascinated by his shape and length, she stroked and gently tugged. He was perfect; the quintessential male. Her legs turned to water, her mind to jelly, her insides to molten lava.

Max felt as if she were turning him inside out, her small hand torturing him with an ecstasy too great to endure, and at the same time, too great to stop. But his patience snapped, and he swept her into his arms and carried her to the bed.

She wrapped her arms around his neck and held on. A wildfire was searing her, depleting all her oxygen and ravaging her remaining inhibitions. She and Max were about to perform the most intimate act a man and a woman could perform together. The other two times she had had sex had been little more than the acts of a curious young girl. But instinctively she knew what was about to happen would be very different, and in some way she couldn't begin to fathom, momentously important. Unwilling to take time to examine her instinctive feeling, unwilling to wait for him, she stripped off her shorts and panties and dropped them over the side of the bed.

For a moment he could only stare at her. Her wine-red hair lay in lustrous waves against skin that gleamed like satin. Her high, round breasts beckoned and made his mouth go dry. The enticing triangle of soft, curly hair at the apex of her long, sleek legs made him begin to shake. "You're exquisite," he said, his voice uneven. "And I've wanted you ever since I laid eyes on you."

Nerves were quivering throughout her body; her blood was singing through her veins. She literally felt as if she were on fire for him. But there was one more thing she needed to say. "Tell me, Max. Tell me this won't be a one-night stand."

He laughed huskily. "Honey, I can guarantee it." With feverish restlessness his hand brushed across her breasts, then slowly smoothed down her flat stomach. She was soft, liquid, and hot, and he was about to give up his freedom to her without a qualm. For a flash of a moment he was astonished at himself, and then the thought vanished as fast as it had come. *She* was what he wanted.

He delved shaking fingers between her legs and probed at her feminine cleft and delicate folds, then went deeper. His eyes darkened at the heated moistness there. She made a sound of pleasure and satisfaction, and his tone of voice echoed her emotions. "You're ready for me."

"If I get any more ready," she said, her voice whispery with need, "I'll explode."

His laugh turned to a groan. "Your habit of saying exactly what's on your mind is going to be the death of me."

She didn't answer, because her mind had gone blank. Magical things were happening inside her. She was shimmering with heat, trembling with desire. She entwined her arms around his neck and opened her mouth for his hard, fierce kiss. Her hips writhed and undulated beneath his touch; her tongue rasped against his. And a deep frustration grew. She slid her hands down his back to his hips and pulled him to her, showing without words what she wanted.

A growl rumbled up from deep in his chest. He'd thought he was happy and fulfilled. Then he had met her and realized he had been so wrong. Now he had this deeply primitive need for her to belong to him. He wanted to bind her to him as tightly and as securely as her invisible strings had already bound him.

He entered her with a powerful thrust, and to

his overwhelming gratification, her body took his full length with an ease that left him breathless. Her velvet tightness closed around him, sheathing him and driving a fire straight to his brain.

"You make me absolutely crazy, Ashley," he muttered roughly, then forgot all about talking. Primal instinct took over. He surged in and out of her, each stroke more powerful, more urgent, than the last.

She turned hot, wild, and demanding; her hips eagerly rose to meet him. An almost unbearable pressure built deep in her womb, then quickly spread to take complete possession of her. She clutched at him and cried out, certain she was about to break apart into a million pieces and wanting it with everything that was in her.

Miraculously he was making her feel a completeness, a joy, and an ecstasy that she had never known. But somewhere in a haze-filled corner of her mind, a small fear lurked that it would be hard for her ever to get enough of him and the way he was making her feel. Then the fear was forgotten as she cried out his name—and she shattered and came apart in his arms.

Heat and light, black fire and pure, shining white ecstasy crashed and seared. He kept her safe, holding her tightly to him, pounding into her, coming apart himself.

Ashley lay cradled against Max, listening to the water as it gently lapped against the side of the boat. Mingled with his deep, even breathing, the sound was like a lullaby to her. She didn't think she had ever felt this comfortable, or this at peace.

*Peace.* Yes, she thought with some amazement, she had finally found the peace she had been seeking when she had taken that marathon journey across the country. Suddenly she giggled.

Max angled his head so that he could look down at her. "What's so funny?"

"I just realized something. I'm good at sex. I'm *actually* good at sex!"

He chuckled, low and husky. "Honey, I've got a news flash for you. You're more than good. You're *spectacular.*"

"Do you really think so?"

He nodded. "Oh, yes."

"Amazing," she murmured. "Absolutely amazing." His hand stroked up and down her arm, lightly trailing heat. She basked in the feel of his touch and let her mind wander. She supposed she was well and truly out of the frying pan and into the fire now. And much to her surprise, it felt wonderful. If only this feeling, Max, and the two of them together, could last. But it wouldn't. It never did.

She sat up, taking the sheet with her, tucking it beneath her arms, and shifting so that she faced him. "There's something very serious we need to talk about."

Smiling, because he knew what was coming, he piled pillows behind him and leaned back against them. "Okay, Ashley, hit me with your best shot."

She flipped a thick, bothersome section of her hair behind her shoulders. "Well, it's just this. We've already agreed that this won't be a one-night stand. Right?"

"Right."

"And we've also talked about how I'd be lousy at a serious relationship, and you said you didn't want one anyway. Right?"

Had it just been this morning that he had said that? "Right."

"And of course there's my drifting problem."

He knew exactly what she was trying to say, but he was enjoying watching her work her way through what she saw as a dilemma. "Drifting problem?"

"You know—I drift."

*Just try it,* he thought. "Oh, yeah, I remember now. You said you tend to get preoccupied and drift on to other things. I understand completely."

Her eyes narrowed slightly. He seemed to be taking this awfully well. "Well, then, good. As long we both understand that we're going to have more than a one-night stand, but less than a serious relationship, and that I could drift away at any time, then—"

"Then there won't be any hard feelings between us when the time comes."

"Right." She chewed on her bottom lip, wondering why she wasn't happier about his agreement. "I mean, it's not as if I plan to drift away anytime soon. I guess you know Mother has some more people coming in, and it may take me some time to convince everyone that there won't be a wedding. And then there's you. I expect we'll be making love some more." When he didn't say anything, she prompted him. "Right?"

His lips quirked. "Right."

She studied him beneath her lashes. Even lying

perfectly still, he had the ability to stir her. There was such a sense of solidity about him, a sense that she could hold on to him forever. She couldn't imagine anyone drifting away from him. Except her. Unfortunately she knew that she eventually would. And even if by some miraculous chance she didn't, he wouldn't want her to stay anyway. Suddenly she was extremely depressed. "When?"

"I beg your pardon?"

"When can we make love again?"

His smile was tender. "Anytime you like."

"Now?"

"Now," he said, and drew her down to him.


"Will you quit laughing," Ashley whispered to Max, laughing herself. She was tiptoeing along the back terrace of the inn with him following close behind her. Dawn had already begun to light the sky, and she was hoping they wouldn't attract any attention.

"I can't help it," he whispered back. "I keep thinking of the picture we're making, two grown people, trying to sneak undetected into a place *I* own."

She stopped and turned, amused but earnest. "I've already explained this to you. Mother and Leona would be shocked if they knew where I'd been and what I'd been doing, not to mention who I'd been doing it with."

"They don't know about the birds and the bees?"

"I'm fully convinced they've each had sex only once, and that was when Roger and I were conceived."

He burst out laughing.

She grinned and pushed him back against a wall. "Will you please stop *laughing*!"

"I'm sorry, but that struck me as funny. All kids think their parents have had sex only once. Or in the case of those who aren't only children, a number exactly equaling them plus their brothers and sisters."

"Yeah, well, I bet I'm close to being right. Think about Mother and Leona's hair."

"Their hair?"

"You don't keep perfectly styled hair day in and day out, as they do, by rolling around in bed and having some man run his fingers through it. It just can't be done. And they've both been named to the Hairstylists' International Best-Coiffed Hair list more than once."

"Hairstylists'—You're kidding me, right?"

She shook her head. "Nope."

"How many times have you been named to that list?" he asked, already knowing the answer.

"None."

"Thank heavens," he said huskily, pulling her to him and sliding his fingers through her hair.

She felt an exciting rush. After the hours they had just spent, she knew every inch of him, and as hard as it was for her to believe, she was eager for more of the intimacy. She leaned against him, treasuring the feel of his hard body, the sensual rasp of his tongue.

When his hands slid down to cup her buttocks, a thrill raced through her. Reluctantly she pulled her mouth from his, and drew her head back so that she could gaze up at him. "We can't do this here. Someone might see us."

"Like I said, I own the place. I can tell everyone to leave." His hands roamed over her bottom with breathtaking familiarity.

"You know you can't do that," she murmured, beginning to wonder why she was protesting.

"Watch me," he said with twinkling eyes, and bent to kiss her again.

She gave a little cry and twisted out of his arms. "Stop that," she said in a loud whisper, "or we're never going to get to our rooms. Now stay right there, while I look and see if anyone's in the lobby." She eased up to a window, peered in, then quickly jerked back. "There's someone at the desk."

"I would hope so," he said, amused. "I pay him a considerable amount to be there."

"Darn. And he's obviously conscientious. Why couldn't he be one of those night clerks who sleep on the job or make love to their girlfriends behind the desk?"

He gave a mock sigh. "Okay, Ashley, tell me the truth. Was one or both of your one-night stands with a night clerk?"

She glared at him. "No! And quit trying to distract me. Now what are we going to do?"

He drew her back to him. "I vote I kiss you again."

"You know," a cool, feminine voice drawled, "you two are making this much more difficult than it has to be."

# *Six*

With a sound of distress Ashley whirled around. But at the sight of the lovely blonde seated in a large fanback rattan chair, she broke into a wide smile. "Jacey!"

She rushed over to her. Jacey, cool and sophisticated, dressed in a timeless beige linen pants suit, rose to receive a big hug.

Ashley released her, stepped back, and eyed her friend with delighted amazement. "Aren't you supposed to be in Aruba or Africa or one of those other countries that start with an *A*? What on earth are you doing out here?"

Jacey laughed. "You mean here at the inn or out here on the terrace?"

"Both. Tell me everything."

"Well, I flew into San Francisco yesterday afternoon, had a late, late dinner with a friend. He took me out on his yacht, and we had champagne and sourdough bread as we sailed beneath the Golden

Gate Bridge. It was nice, but not nice enough to stay, so I requested a change of course, returned to terra firma, then rented a car and drove on up here. I checked in about an hour ago, but I wasn't really tired, so since I've never seen a California sunrise before, I decided to delay going to my room until I had to."

"You're staying here! That's great!"

"I suggest you wait until you've heard the answer to the second part of your question before you decide if you think it's so great or not. You're right, by the way. I was going to an *A* country. Australia. But your mother placed this SOS call to me just hours before I was supposed to leave, and asked me to come here instead."

"Why?"

"Something to do with being a bridesmaid."

"Oh." She glanced over her shoulder at Max. He was still leaning against the wall, his arms crossed, his eyes narrowed on her. She looked back at Jacey. "And you abandoned Australia, just like that?"

Jacey's normally icy aqua eyes twinkled with warmth. "It's not going anywhere. Besides, it was getting more and more obvious that all the excitement seemed to be here. And I must say, from what little I've seen so far, I was right." She gave Ashley a significant look, then strolled over to Max and held out her hand. "Hi. I'm Jacey Killane, an old friend of Ashley's."

Smiling, he straightened and took her hand. "I'm Max Hayden. Welcome."

Jacey laughed. "Thanks. So far, I'm having a great time."

He slid his hands into his trouser pockets, perfectly at ease. "We aim to please."

"By the way, I can vouch for what Ashley said about Miriam and Leona. They've each had sex once each, and that's it."

Ashley had followed Jacey and was pleased to see that she and Max seemed to like each other. She hadn't doubted that Max would like Jacey—all men did. She had a cool, refined, untouchable beauty that drove men to want to possess her. But Jacey was finicky, and Ashley had seen her freeze out many men. "Jacey and I have been friends forever," she said to Max.

Jacey nodded. "That's right. We started at Miss Abigail's School for Young Ladies when we were four. It was sort of a prekindergarten finishing school."

Ashley made a face. "Jacey graduated. I flunked out."

Jacey lightly touched a perfectly manicured hand to Max's sleeve. "That's because Miss Abigail was a stickler for little white gloves, and Ashley could never learn which one went on which hand."

Max chuckled and Ashley grimaced. "Miss Abigail and Mother both tried everything, but I just couldn't get the knack of wearing them. I did like to chew on them, though. I'm afraid the signs were there early that I wasn't cut out to be society's idea of a lady."

"Thank heaven," Max murmured, his eyes on her.

A light rose hue tinted Ashley's cheeks.

Jacey's interested gaze went from Max to Ashley and then back to Max. "I hope you don't mind my interrupting you two, but I couldn't resist trying to help. The solution to your problem seems so simple. Max, if Miriam sees you, you can tell her you've been jogging, and Ashley, you can tell her you couldn't sleep, went for a drive, and got lost."

"You're right. That would be the simple solution. The thing is, I hate to lie to Mother."

"She also hates to tell her mother no," Max said pointedly.

"Don't start, Max."

His expression was amazingly close to angelic. "I never stopped, Ashley."

Just then a waiter walked out, carrying a tray, and placed it on a nearby table.

"Wonderful, my coffee's here," Jacey said. "You two come join me."

Ashley gnawed on her lower lip. "I don't know. Mother and Leona are probably already up. Even on vacation, they keep to their schedule."

"Except," Max said, moving over to the table and taking a chair, "they're not on vacation, they're here on a mission. And yes, Jacey, we'll be glad to join you."

With a smile Jacey took the ticket from the waiter, signed it, and handed it back to him. "Could you please bring out another cup, an extra pot of coffee, and a Coke?" With a nod the waiter hurried off.

Ashley sank into one of the chairs, plucked a sugar cube from a small silver bowl, and nibbled on it. "As you can no doubt tell, Jacey, the wedding is a bone of contention between Max and me."

"Yes, and now I'm positive I made the right

decision to postpone Australia. I'm dying to know what's going on with you two."

"Nothing," Ashley said quickly. "Well, not exactly nothing. What I mean is, Max owns the inn, and I'm staying here, and we met, and he has this boat, and—"

Their waiter appeared with their order and looked at Max. "Shall I serve?"

"We'll do it." He poured Ashley's Coke into a glass full of ice, handed it to her, then helped himself to the coffee.

Jacey waited to speak until the waiter had left. "Max, is there anything you'd care to add to Ashley's interpretation of things?"

He sipped at his coffee and smiled at Ashley. "I think she pretty much said it all."

"She said exactly nothing, but I can accept that. For now. So tell me, how are the plans for the wedding going so far?"

"Beautifully," Max said sarcastically. "Things are rolling right along. In fact, last night Sybella picked the date. It's to be the third Saturday in September."

Jacey grinned. "Gee, Ashley, I don't know. I may be booked up that weekend. I'll have to check my calendar."

Ashley kicked her under the table. "Watch out, or I'll tell Mother you want a pink bridesmaid dress."

"You wouldn't!"

"I would."

"No way. Pink makes me bilious. I absolutely will not, under any circumstances, wear pink. So if you want me to be a bridesmaid—by the way, *do* you want me to be a bridesmaid at your wedding?"

"Of course I do." Out of the corner of her eye she saw Max's eyebrows shoot up. "What I actually mean is that *if* I were to ever get married—which I cannot in my wildest imagination see me doing—but *if* I were to ever get married, you would be at the top of my list. In fact, you would be my maid of honor."

Jacey nodded with satisfaction. "Good, because I'd like to think I could add a few nuances to the job, maybe give *maid* a whole new meaning."

Miriam and Leona burst through the doors, crisp in their tennis whites and smiling broadly. Ashley tensed and swallowed the sugar cube.

"Jacey, darling, you're here at last!"

Jacey rose and received a kiss and a hug from each of the women. "Sorry I'm a little late. I stopped over in San Francisco."

Leona patted her hand. "All that matters is that you're here now. You're going to be such a big help. Hello, Mr. Hayden. What a nice surprise to find you out here this morning with our two girls."

"Good morning, Mr. Hayden," Miriam said, bestowing a gracious smile on him before turning to Jacey. "Leona's right. We're awfully glad you decided to put Australia on the back burner for a while."

"It would take a huge stove to do that," Ashley muttered.

The peace she had found with Max last night on his boat was gone. Illogically she felt as if she were five years old again and had just been caught with her hand in the cookie jar. But then she had never had to face her mother after spending a night of mind-warping passion with a man. It was unnerving. And the fact that the man was still at her side made it all the worse. Much to her chagrin, she was totally rattled. She braced for the inevitable.

Miriam's brow creased with concern as she turned her attention to her daughter. "Darling, you have on the same outfit you wore yesterday."

Ashley glanced down at herself. "I-I really like it. It's perfect for here, don't you agree?"

"It's nice—a little bare, but you look lovely in it, perfectly lovely. I must say, though, I'm a little surprised to see you out and about so early. Did you just happen to run into Mr. Hayden and Jacey?"

Her mind raced as she tried to remember what Jacey had suggested. She hated having to lie to her mother once again. "Uh, yes, I couldn't sleep, and so I got up and went for a jog, and—"

Max made a quiet choking sound, and Jacey reached for her coffee.

Realizing immediately that she had used the wrong excuse, she grabbed another subject out of the air to cover her mistake. "Jacey, you'll have to check out the boutique here in the inn. They have the greatest things. Very California, which is appropriate, since that's where we are. . . . Ummm . . ."

Jacey took up the slack and turned to Max. "I'm glad to hear about the boutique. I'm registered as a preferred customer in stores all over the world." He grinned. "I'll put on extra help."

A frown had appeared on Miriam's subtly made-up face. "Darling, you've never jogged in your life."

"I know, but it must be this wonderful sea air. It's so invigorating, don't you agree?"

"And you're barefoot."

Was it too much to ask that maybe one of these days someone would agree with her? "I'm what?" She glanced down at her feet. "Oh, that's right, I couldn't find my shoes, and I was in a hurry—" What was she doing? She was talking about something that had happened last night! She had to get a grip on herself.

"Why were you in such a hurry?"

Leona saved her from answering by speaking up. "You really should have the proper shoes if you're going to take up jogging, Ashley. Maybe we can go into town later on today and buy you some."

"Oh, no, that won't be necessary, I'll—"

"Mr. Hayden," Miriam said, "are you an early riser?"

With a shrug and a mischievous grin, Max took the remaining excuse. "Not usually, but I couldn't sleep, so I took a drive and got lost."

Ashley slid down in the chair, and Jacey suddenly took an interest in her nails.

"Lost? Don't you live here year round?" Leona asked.

His eyes gleamed. "Yes, but sometimes these California nights offer unexpected surprises, and you can end up going places you've never been before."

Ashley stripped and stepped into the shower. She had finally managed to make a graceful exit from the scene down on the terrace. At least she hoped it had been graceful. She had pleaded weariness and claimed she was in desperate need of a nap. And she hadn't been lying.

She closed her eyes, feeling the water beat down on her, unknotting nerves and dissolving tension.

Max. What was she going to do about him? Or maybe, she thought, it would be more correct to ask what she was going to do about herself. But she was confused and couldn't seem to sort through her feelings.

After last night, she would never be the same again. She could feel the change in herself. There was an awareness in her that had never been there before. And an aching for a vague, undefined something that somehow she knew she would never have.

Maybe it would have been better if last night never happened. She had been swamped and consumed by their passion. Max had had her clinging to him, time and time again, crying out his name. And now he was all she could think about.

The shower door opened, and then Max was there with her, naked, looking at her with eyes that burned with a desire he had made her all too familiar with.

"I was wondering if you could use some help in washing your back."

She grinned, somewhat amazed at her sudden shyness. "What you were really wondering is why I came unglued down there on the terrace. Right?"

"Wrong. And you didn't come unglued. You did fine."

Her grin widened. "Oh, sure I did."

"You did."

"I felt as if the words 'I've just spent the night having sex' were emblazoned across my forehead."

"Well, they weren't. And if you want to know the truth, I wasn't wondering whether you needed some help with your back. I was *hoping*, because, Ashley, I really need to help you."

It never occurred to her to say no. She could already feel her body softening, heating. "I'm glad you're here. I do need . . ."

He shifted so that he wasn't blocking the steam of water from her and turned her so that she faced away from him. He soaped a washcloth, then began to gently rub her back.

Almost immediately she was filled with an insidious pleasure. He slid the sensually rough terry cloth over her water-slick body, arousing nerves to tingling life. And when he skimmed the cloth down her spine to circle over her buttocks, she placed her palms and forearms against the tile wall and leaned against it for support.

Letting the steam and the heat envelop her, she ceased thinking.

He pushed her soaking hair to one side of her neck so he could kiss the other side, and reached around her, lathering the front of her body. As he pressed against her, his chest hair grazed her back, creating a new and additional tantalizing sensation. Her breasts tightened; a heavy throb started between her legs. Unconsciously she widened her stance, inviting him to ease the excruciatingly wonderful pain. He obliged, abandoning the washcloth, and using his fingers. She moaned, unable to help herself. His hardened maleness nudged, his fingers delved and stroked her soft female folds.

To her it was incomprehensible that she should want him again after the night of almost unrelenting lovemaking they had just spent. But she did.

Using what little strength she had remaining, she turned. Before she even had to ask, he cupped her buttocks, lifted her, and drove into her.


Max raised himself up on one elbow and gazed down at Ashley, who was still sleeping. She lay on her stomach, the sheet down around her waist. Early afternoon light slipped through the drapes and layered her skin with a luminescence and threaded a shine through her wine-colored hair. Very gently, he brushed back the hair that had fallen across her face so he could see her.

His heart swelled with love as he gazed at her. She was so beautiful, so breathtakingly precious to him. He could still see those invisible strings of hers, but they no longer concerned him. He was well and truly tangled in them now, bound to her irrevocably, and he had no intention of trying to escape. Ever.

He hadn't known that anyone could be so stimulating and fun until he had met Ashley. He hadn't known a woman could make him want her constantly.

He pressed a light kiss on her shoulder, then pulled the sheet up until it covered her. He knew she wasn't going to marry Roger, because he wasn't going to let her. But he had a definite problem. How in the world was he going to keep her from drifting away from him?

One thing was for damned sure: He was going to come up with something.

A loud knocking sound tugged at Ashley through thick clouds of sleep. She rolled over and drifted back to sleep. The sound came again. This time she woke up enough to realize that someone *was* knocking on her door. It was probably the maid, she thought groggily. But she'd go away. She had put the security lock on, and the maid wouldn't be able to get in.

"Ashley, darling! Are you still asleep?"

She sat straight up in bed. *"Mother?"*

"Ashley, are you all right? Open the door."

"Be right there," she called, and hurtled out of bed. Then she stopped and looked back at the rumpled covers. "Max?"

Where was he? She felt a brief pang of disappointment. He had been holding her when she had fallen asleep. Had he left? And if so why? She glanced toward the French doors. They were closed and the drapes were drawn, just as they had been when they had come out of the shower after making love and had fallen asleep. Maybe he had heard the knock before she had and decided to hide so as not to embarrass her.

"Max," she said in a magnified whisper, "are you in here?"

*"Ashley!"*

"Coming, Mother." She started for the door, then stopped again. She was naked! She raced into the bathroom, yanked her bathrobe from a hook on the back of the door, then, as an afterthought, jerked open the shower curtain. No Max. Where was he? She hurried to the door.

Her mother walked in, the scent of Estée Lauder trailing behind her. She looked as fresh as a daisy in slim white pants, a red silk blouse, and discreet gold jewelry. "Darling, when you said you were coming up to take a nap, I had no idea you'd sleep this long."

"I guess I was more tired than I thought."

"That's understandable after what you've just done."

For a minute she panicked. She had always heard that mothers had a way of knowing everything. "What I've just done?" she asked carefully.

"I know you wanted the adventure of driving across the country, but it must have been grueling for you."

"Oh that." Relieved, she pushed the door shut. "It was tiring, but I enjoyed it."

Her mother smiled lovingly. "I'm glad. I guess it's important to have one last little fling before a girl settles down."

Ashley groaned and sank down on the end of the bed. "How many times am I going to have to tell you before you'll believe me that I'm not marrying Roger?"

Her mother sat down beside her and took her hand in hers. "I know you think I'm not taking your protests seriously, but the truth is I'm taking them very seriously. I understand all about prewedding jitters. I had them myself before I married your father."

"You did?" Ashley asked, diverted by the comment.

Her mother patted her hand. "Of course I did. I remember it so clearly. For a week before the wedding I couldn't eat or sleep. Then the day of the wedding arrived, and there I was in the bride's room located at the back of the church. I was so scared, I almost climbed out the window and left. To this day I'm convinced that if I'd done it, I would have made a clean getaway."

Ashley grinned, delighted at the idea that her mother had actually contemplated doing something so unorthodox as escaping from a church full of people on her wedding day, not to mention her very proper father. "What kept you from it?"

Her mother smiled. "I loved your father. And not once in the thirty years that he and I have been married have I regretted walking down that aisle. And you won't either. You'll see. Trust me." She rose and strolled toward the French doors.

"But, Mother, what I feel for Roger is different from what you felt for Dad—" Her eyes widened with alarm, and she bolted off the bed. "What are you *doing*?"

"I'm just looking for the pull cord. I thought I'd let in a little light."

"I'll do it." She waited until her mother had moved away, then peered behind the drapes. In movies people always hid behind drapes, but she supposed Max hadn't seen the same movies she had because he wasn't there. She pulled the cord, and the drapes opened.

"You've always loved Roger, I know you have."

"Yes, but it's a different kind of love."

"But don't you see, darling, that's the beauty of love. It grows with the years. Believe me, I know what I'm talking about. In years to come you'll thank me. You know, this is really a lovely room. Do you have secure locks?"

She chewed on her bottom lip. "Yes."

"This inn is a little jewel of a place. I can't wait to get home and tell my friends."

"I'm sure Max will appreciate that." She glanced at the bed. She supposed he could be hiding under it. She'd check after her mother had gone. Maybe she'd even find her shoes.

Miriam glanced at herself in the mirror and adjusted an already straight collar. "Listen, darling, get dressed and come downstairs as soon as you can. We need you. The caterer has arrived, and we're expecting Jean Marc at any time. We were so fortunate that he agreed to fly out here on such short notice, but you know how much he's always liked you. He's promised to bring some fabulous designs, and I can't wait to see them."

"Mother, I don't want to hurt you, but I'm not getting married."

Smiling, her eyes misty with tears of love, her mother walked over to her, reached up, and took her face between her hands. "My beautiful little girl. You have been the light of my life since the day you were born. Please don't worry. Everything is going to work out splendidly. You'll see."

# *Seven*

Ashley gloomily contemplated the contents of her closet, mentally eliminating the things that her mother and Leona had brought her. Her mother had said they needed her, but at the moment she just didn't feel up to listening to plans for a wedding that wasn't going to happen. She had been in California three days, and she hadn't even been on the beach yet. Today, she decided, was going to be the day.

She chose a swimsuit that was abloom with lush tropical colors of olive green, orange, yellow, purple, and magenta. The top was strapless and dipped into a deep U between her breasts. The bikini bottom had high-cut legs that made her already impossibly long legs appear even longer. The last touch was a sarong skirt with an asymmetrical hem that she wrapped around her waist and tied at the side. Sandals and a thick gold bracelet completed her outfit.

After carelessly combing her fingers through the thick waves of her hair, she left the room and took the stairs down to the lobby. The sight that greeted her was nothing short of astounding.

The usual quiet and serenity of the lobby was gone. All sorts of people milled about. Bellboys and assorted staff hurried here and there, pushing carts filled with luggage and traveling trunks.

Jean Marc—tall, dark-haired, patrician—stood in the middle of the fray, wearing his habitual expression of hauteur and keeping a commanding eye on the cart that held big leather sketch cases. No doubt Pierre Lavosier—caterer, chef, and baker extraordinaire to society's elite—was also somewhere in the crowd, but he was too short for her to spot.

Marge was at the reception desk, trying to deal with several people at once. A few of the "normal" guests, as Ashley mentally called those people who were not imported from New York by her mother, sat to the side, watching with the same expression they might have watching a circus show. And to make matters worse, a telephone was ringing somewhere, and *no* one was answering it!

Plowing through the crowd, Ashley headed in the direction of the phone. She tried to keep calm, telling herself that someone was bound to answer it, but its shrill sound grew louder as she neared it. By the time she reached the reception desk, her teeth were gritted and her jaw was hurting. "Marge, do you think you could answer the phone?"

Marge was staring hard at a computer screen

while listening to two people who [...]
her at once. And the phone kept r[...]

Couldn't anyone hear the phone[...]

It rang again. She bolted aroun[...]
jerked up the phone. "Hello? Plea[...]
morrow. You don't have a chance of being helped
today." She slammed the phone down, feeling
much better. It rang again. She lifted the receiver
and placed it crosswise across the cradle.

Max. Where was Max? Her eyes scanned the
lobby several times before she saw him. He was
sitting in a corner, talking with her mother and
Leona. She could only imagine how furious he
must be at the way his inn had been taken over.

Her mind took a sharp turn in a new direction,
and her heart leaped into her throat. Oh, *no!* He
was so against the wedding, he might tell her
mother and Leona what they'd done this morning,
not to mention last night!

As she hurried over to them, she noticed with
horror that her mother was writing in the small
burgundy leather organizer she took with her
everywhere. She actually looked as if she was
taking notes on what he was telling them! She
would probably end up writing a book and call it
*Daughter Dearest.*

Or maybe *My Daughter's Virginity—Gone With
the Wind.*

Her mother didn't know her virginity had gone
with the wind years before. . . .

Her mother looked up with a smile. "Oh, good,
darling, you're finally here. But why are you
dressed like that? We have work to do."

She could feel the heat of Max's gaze as it

...med over her, taking in what she was wear-
... If the intensity of the heat she was feeling was
anything to go by, he liked the outfit. But right
now, she was too worried to be pleased. "I don't
have any work to do, Mother. I'm here on vacation,
and I'm going to spend the afternoon on the
beach."

"I suppose we could do without her for one or
two hours," Leona said to Miriam, then smiled at
Ashley. "But be sure and wear plenty of sunscreen.
I don't think brides show to their best advantage
when they have too much of a tan."

She felt like screaming. Instead, she calmly
asked Max, "May I please speak with you?" When
he didn't move, she added, "Privately."

"Certainly."

She expected a question or at least a comment
from her mother about why she wanted to speak to
him privately, but much to her surprise, her
mother said nothing.

He stood. "Ladies, I enjoyed our little talk."

"We did too," Miriam said. "And thank you so
much for your time and help."

"It was my pleasure." He turned and looked at
Ashley. "Where would you like to talk?"

She glanced around and saw a vacant seating
arrangement across the room. "Over there." As
soon as they reached one of the couches and were
seated, she asked the question that was upper-
most in her mind. "Just exactly what kind of help
did you give them?"

His eyebrows lifted. "You sound as if you're
accusing me of something."

"No, no." She rubbed her forehead. "Well, it did

occur to me that you might tell them about what we've done."

"Oh, you mean tell them that we spent last night and a good portion of this morning tangled up together on various surfaces, driving each other out of our minds with our lovemaking?"

"Shhh!" Alarmed, she glanced around to see if anyone had heard.

"I wouldn't tell them, Ashley."

"Maybe you wouldn't on purpose, but you might be talking along, and your mind would be on something else, and suddenly you've said the wrong thing." She shrugged. "It happens to me all the time."

"I'll try to watch what I say," he said solemnly.

"Good." Lord, he was well-nigh irresistible when his eyes twinkled as they were doing now. Or when fire burned in their depths. "Where did you go? When I fell asleep, you were there, and when I woke up, you were gone."

"Were you disappointed?"

His deep voice sent warmth skidding through her.

"No, of course not." But she had been, she remembered. Maybe that was why she had wanted to think that he was hiding in the room somewhere rather than that he had deserted her. "It's just that Mother was at the door, and I thought—"

"I'm sorry I left, Ashley. But if I'd stayed, I wasn't sure I would have been able to keep my hands off you, and you wouldn't have gotten as much sleep as you did. Plus, there were some things I had to see to."

His explanation made her feel better, though she

wasn't sure she wanted to admit it, especially not to herself. "I have an apology to make to you too. I'm really sorry for the chaos my mother and Leona have caused in your inn. Poor Marge doesn't even have time to answer the phone. I'm afraid I ended up taking it off the hook."

"Don't worry about it. I've arranged for Cameron to come in early and assist Marge."

"But in the meantime you may lose business because the phone is off the hook."

"I think I've got all the business I can handle, don't you? Besides, it won't be long before we have everything organized. I was just helping Miriam and Leona sort out a few logistics, telling them where their people could set up, that sort of thing."

"You really were helping them! As in *helping*?"

"Sure. Why not?"

"Well, because—" Her mind switched course midsentence. "You're calling them Miriam and Leona now?"

"They asked me to."

"They asked—"

"Those colors look absolutely outrageous on you."

Her brow pleated. "You don't like them?"

"I love them, especially in combination with your hair. Orange, purple, magenta, and masses of wine. You look outrageously beautiful, and I want you again."

The breath left her lungs. "Max—"

The waiter who had served her breakfast the first morning she had been at the inn hurried up to them. "Max, you need to come quick. War has broken out in the kitchen. There's a Frenchman in there trying to take over Greta's kitchen, and she's mad as all hell."

"I'd better go with you," Ashley said. "I know who the Frenchman is."

It was just as she had thought. When she and Max reached the kitchen, she found the diminutive Pierre Lavosier. He was clutching a leather attaché case to his chest, staring with wonder and admiration at the imposing six-foot Greta, head chef of the inn, as she hurled insults and abuse at him.

Greta's expression lightened when she saw Max. "Thank goodness you're here! This little weasel thinks he's going to barge in and take over my kitchen."

Pierre's eyes widened with distress. "But, *no*! I am not here to barge."

She took a step closer, towering over him. "And just exactly what do you have in that case? What are you trying to smuggle in here?"

"*Mademoiselle!* I have my own special spices in zis case, plus my own blend of vanilla, grown on a plantation personally inspected yearly by me. I carry zis case with me everywhere. People would commit *kill* to know my secret ingredients!"

"I'm going to commit kill if you don't get out of here."

"Greta," Max said. "I think we can work something out here. I'm sure he will agree to stay out of the kitchen during peak hours. As for the rest of the time, perhaps you can give him a corner of the kitchen and one oven."

Why was he trying to be so helpful? Ashley wondered, slightly annoyed.

Fearlessly Pierre straightened to his full five-foot height. "The gentleman is correct. There is no need to commit kiil. I am here merely to create a few masterpieces for zee bride to taste and to decide upon." He darted across the room to Ashley. "*Here*. See for yourself. Here is zee bride. She will tell you." He looked at her. "Tell her."

"I am not zee, I mean *the*, bride, Pierre, and I'm afraid this isn't going to work."

"No, no, you are wrong. It must work! I must create in zis beautiful kitchen, alongside zis beautiful woman."

Greta folded her arms beneath her ample bosom and gazed menacingly at him. "Who are you calling a beautiful woman, you little shrimp?"

"*Sacre bleu*, it is you! *You*, my magnificent one! You are as full-bodied as one of our finest French wines, as architecturally perfect as our beloved Eiffel Tower. If you were in France, men would worship you." He suddenly knelt on one knee. "I myself fall at your feet now, zis moment."

Greta unfolded her arms and looked at him with new interest. "Worship?"

Ashley reached down and pulled Pierre to his feet. "I saw quite a few drivers in the lobby. Let's go find one, get your bags loaded up, and you can be back in New York by tonight."

Greta held up one large hand. "It's possible that we might be able to work something out. As long as the little shrimp understands that there is only one boss in this kitchen, and that is *me*."

Pierre's thin face broke out into a wide smile. "But of course!"

Max rubbed his hands together. "Good, I'm glad we were able to work things out."

"Wait a minute," Ashley said, bewildered.

Max's hand closed around her upper arm. "We should get out of here and let Pierre settle in." He led her out of the kitchen, through the dining room, and back into the crowded lobby. "You see that large potted palm over there?" he asked.

Still trying to figure out why he had handled the situation in the kitchen the way he had, she followed his gaze to where a large, full palm sat in front of a paneled wall. "Yes. Why?"

"Because I'm going to go over there and disappear behind it, and in a minute, I want you to follow me."

Her brows drew together. "Excuse me?"

"Just do it."

While she counted to sixty seconds, she scanned the crowd and was grateful to see that her mother and Leona didn't seem to be anywhere in sight. However, BoBo was standing by the reception desk, speaking animatedly to several people. And through the windows she could see Sybella sitting in the lotus position out on the beach, no doubt meditating.

When she reached sixty, she crossed the room to the palm, wondering what in the world Max was up to. Much to her surprise, she found ample space between the wall and the palm. But Max wasn't there. And then a door in the paneled wall opened, his arm came out, and he pulled her into a lighted, large room lined with tall, deep shelves.

"Max! What are you doing? Where are we?"

"Sssh, not so loud. Anyone who walks by can hear us. We're in the luggage-holding room."

"Oh." She looked around her. "There's only one set of luggage in here."

"That's because only one person has checked out today. He's probably taking a last walk on the beach or maybe having an early dinner before he sets out for his next destination."

So far, everything sounded reasonable to her. "Okay, but what are we doing here?"

"This." He hooked his finger into the U of her swimsuit top, pulled her against him, and buried his face in the curve of her scented neck. "I told you I wanted you again."

And she wanted him, she thought with amazement. Desire flickered darkly in his eyes, and she felt an answering flicker inside her. But again? And *here*? "We've already made love once today," she said, breathless from his lips nibbling her throat and the lobe of her ear. "Well, probably more than that if you count what we did on the boat after midnight, and, uh, I guess technically we should count—"

He claimed her mouth with a hunger that made her forget the rest of what she had been about to say. He kissed her with an urgency that she couldn't help but respond to. It was an exciting, raw, very basic kind of kiss, the kind that was all tongue and teeth and straining to get closer. By the time he lifted his head, fires had ignited all through her body, and her arms were circled tightly around his neck.

"I didn't mean to do this," he said, sliding his hand beneath the sarong to the tight-fitting bottom of the bikini. "I meant to stop with the kiss, but . . ." He pushed the bikini bottom down her legs and freed one of her feet.

She gasped. "What are you doing? Whoever owns those suitcases could come back at any moment."

"It's a chance I'm willing to take. What about you?"

A roaring started in her ears. Heat looped into knots in her stomach and tightened. The decision was hers. Or had she already made the decision? "We shouldn't."

"You're probably right," he murmured. "But I may explode if I don't have you right this minute. So let's explode together."

Desire and excitement gripped her, sensations too strong to deny trapped her. Unsure of what she wanted to say, she whispered the one word that made sense. "Max."

She wasn't certain how it had happened, but need for him had become a constant in her blood-stream, and at the moment there appeared to be only one thing she could do about it.

He pulled a packing quilt from a shelf, spread it on the floor, then lowered her onto it. Quickly he unzipped his pants, then entered her.

A great surge of heat rolled through her, pene-trating and infiltrating to the very substance of everything that was her.

"We won't stay in here long," he muttered. "I promise. I just had to be inside you for a few minutes. "I *missed* you, your feel, your taste. Lord, tell me you don't mind."

"No," she whispered. *Heavens* no. Whenever he

was in her, wherever they were, even in this luggage closet, she felt as if she were in the exact spot in the universe that she should be. There were no thoughts of drifting or getting lost. There were only thoughts of Max and of the pleasure and the rapture.

At first he lay still. "Absolutely amazing," he whispered hoarsely. "You're hot inside and out." His hand caressed her breast; his lips gently brushed back and forth across hers.

In one small, distant part of her mind, she heard the murmur of people talking on the other side of the wall; occasionally she even recognized a voice. But their nearness seemed unimportant.

His mouth, his hand, his being inside her, were drawing her down into a whirlpool of desire, and Max was its center. *Her* center.

He felt a fierce sense of masculine satisfaction when her hips began to move beneath his. Her pelvis lifted, twisting and writhing. If he'd been a stronger man where she was concerned, he might have remained still and enjoyed the unique sensation of her taking him, but it was an impossibility. He thrust into her, hard, stroking deeply, strongly.

She began to tremble as she neared her crest. He covered her mouth with his when he heard her first moan, wanting the next sounds for his very own.


The afternoon sun was a great golden ball hanging low in the sky as Ashley made her way out to the deserted beach. She strolled along the sand, walking far enough so that no one glancing out one of the windows would be able to see her. Then, the sarong floating out around her, she sat down.

She watched the waves spill onto the shore, one after the other, and wondered why her life couldn't be as consistent. She had long understood that there were people who thought her lifestyle irregular and perhaps even a trifle unorthodox. It had never bothered her before, but now for some reason it was beginning to.

What was wrong with her? What was happening to her?

Heaven help her, she'd just made love in a closet. Okay, she silently amended, a luggage-holding room. But what difference did it make? She had turned into a wanton.

She searched her heart and mind for some sign of remorse concerning this new development in her character. There was nothing. She sighed. She should be ashamed of herself for not feeling at least a *little* conscience-stricken. But she didn't.

One man had somehow rearranged the marrow of her bones so that she throbbed and ached for him as she never had for any other.

"You look deep in thought. Would you like some company, or would you rather be alone?"

Ashley glanced up and saw Jacey. "Pull up a piece of sand and sit down."

"Are you sure?"

"Yeah. I was deep in thought, but I'm not getting anywhere. I suppose the problem is, I'm not sure where I'm supposed to be going. As usual."

Jacey sank down beside her. "Let me guess. It's got something to do with that gorgeous man you were sneaking into the inn with this morning."

"No. Well, yes, I guess it does. Actually it definitely does." She thought for a minute. "I suppose we're having what you would call an affair."

"You don't know?"

"It's a little complicated. You see, I didn't want to have a one-night stand, and neither one of us wants a serious relationship, so that means we're having something that falls in between those two things. Like an affair. Right?"

"Let's see," Jacey said thoughtfully. "I think most people would loosely define an affair as a passionate attachment of limited duration."

"Then I guess that's what we're having—a passionate attachment of limited duration." The limited duration part didn't make her too happy. How limited was limited? Suddenly she burst out laughing. "Leave it to you to give me a definition."

"Wasn't that what you were trying to do?"

"I suppose, but I envy you, Jacey. You've always had such an organized mind. You've never had a broken nail in your life." She held out her hand so Jacey could see her broken nails. "And you've never in your life had any trouble making people understand when you said no."

Just for a moment Jacey's icy aqua eyes clouded, darkened. "Don't envy me, Ashley. In fact, don't envy anyone. You're a beautiful person both inside and out and have more going for you than most of the people I know. Don't let anyone ever tell you differently."

Ashley reached over and gave Jacey a quick hug. "Thanks."

"You're welcome, but what's with this sudden

doubting and questioning? You've never done it before."

Ashley grinned ruefully. "I know, but then I've never had an inn full of people with all their brain waves directed as one toward trying to get me to the altar."

"You're not worried about them, are you?"

"No, not really."

"Then what is it?"

Ashley dug her toes into the sand. "Max."

"Just as I thought. The gorgeous Max. What could be so worrying about him? As far as I can see, he's quite wonderful."

Ashley threw up her hands, disgusted with herself. "He is. I don't know what's wrong with me or what's worrying me." She fell silent for a moment. "Jacey?"

"Ummm?"

"You know how you like to do things you've never done before?"

"Yes."

"Well, when Max and I . . . uh, when we're together—"

"You mean like you were in the luggage-holding room a little while ago?"

"You saw us go in there!"

Jacey's eyes twinkled. "I saw you come out, but don't worry. No one else did. Go on."

"Okay, well, yeah, like when we were in the luggage closet, I mean, holding room. Remember how I used to tell you how lousy at sex I was?" Jacey nodded. "Well, I'm not anymore. I'm *great*."

Jacey's eyes widened. "*Congratulations!*"

Ashley grinned, then her grin faded. "The thing

is, he's liable to take off for Cabo San Lucas at any time. And I'm not ready for him to leave."

"I've seen the way he looks at you, honey. I don't think there's any way he's going to leave until you're ready to go back to New York, or wherever it is that you want to go next."

"Yeah, maybe you're right." The thing was, she was beginning to wonder whether she would ever be ready to leave here. Leave him. She had only been away from him for about an hour, and already she was feeling an urgency to get back to him. "Any new developments back at the inn with the wedding planners?"

"When I slipped out, Sybella was going around asking everyone from me to Pierre to the mothers what their signs were. Seems she's very concerned that everyone who's involved with the wedding have planets that are compatible. Apparently colliding planets would be very bad."

"I don't see how it could help being bad! Maybe Mother should call in Carl Sagan."

Jacey laughed. "She even asked Max, because the wedding is being planned at his inn."

Ashley groaned. "I bet he loved that."

"Actually he was very nice to her and gave her all the information she wanted." Jacey glanced back toward the inn. "Uh-oh. BoBo is on the terrace, waving at us."

Ashley looked over her shoulder and saw what Jacey was talking about. In her eagerness to communicate with them, Bobo was moving her arms in strange patterns. "She looks as if she's giving signals at sea, doesn't she? She just needs the proper flags. I wonder if she's ever had a class in semaphoring?"

Jacey waved back and yelled, "We'll be there in a minute. Ashley, if you don't want all the troops down here, you'd better go in."

Ashley sighed. "Will you do me a favor?"

"Name it."

"Can you think of some way to keep them all busy tonight?"

"Boy, you don't ask small favors, do you?"

Ashley shook her head. "I know it'll be hard. Offhand I can't think of anything that would keep all of them busy at the same time, but if anyone can do it, you can."

"I gather," Jacey said dryly, "that this effort I'm about to put forth is so that you and Max can slip off somewhere together."

"You gather correctly. I want to be with him, but at the same time, I don't want Mother and Leona to get hurt. I've been trying to prevent that for some time now."

"I know you have. When did you start? About a week after the engagement party?"

"Something like that."

"By the way, it was a great engagement party."

"Yes, it was, wasn't it? As I recall, I thought we were all supposed to be attending a quiet little dinner that night. I still don't know how I got so mixed up, but I forgot about being annoyed when I saw all my friends. You have to hand it to Mother and Leona, they know how to entertain so everyone has fun."

"Yes," Jacey said thoughtfully. "And I guess that's just what I have to do tonight. I'm not sure what I'll be able to come up with, but I promise I'll definitely think of something."

"Thanks, Jacey."

"Hey, you know me. I'm a sucker for a good cause."

Later that evening Jacey stood by the front door of the inn, directing her troops. "Come on, everybody. We have vans and cars out front; just pick one and hop in."

On his way, Jean Marc paused by her side, puzzlement on his face. "Where exactly is it that you're taking us?"

"It's a surprise, but I guarantee this will be one of the most unique experiences of your life. You may even come back with inspiration for a new fashion line."

"That's quite a tall order, Jacey. It will be interesting to see if you can deliver."

She gave a mock sound of affront. "Jean Marc, I can't believe you're doubting me."

He smiled. "You're right. Of all people, I shouldn't doubt you." His attention was caught by Sybella, who was just walking out the door, her laptop computer tucked within the folds of her garment. "Sybella, let's take the same van. I need you to pick out a date for me for a trip I have to take to Paris next month."

Jacey turned and saw a sour-faced Greta and a beaming Pierre approaching. "Greta, I'm so glad Pierre was able to talk you into coming."

"The little twerp wouldn't leave me alone until I said I would."

"You won't be sorry. We're going to have a lot of fun."

Jean Marc's and Pierre's assistants passed by; then she saw BoBo, Miriam, and Leona. "Ladies, I hope you're all up for a great time tonight."

Leona chuckled. "This is already fun. I've never gone somewhere and not known my destination in advance."

"And the fun's not going to stop there. I promise you that you ladies will be the envy of all your friends when you get back to New York and tell them about tonight."

BoBo had a slight frown on her face. "At least give us a clue. Have we ever done this before?"

"I would put it into a contract that you haven't."

"What about you, Jacey?" Miriam asked, fishing through her handbag to make sure she had everything she might need.

"I've never done it before either. It's why I thought of it in the first place, and I can't wait. Now is everyone loaded up?"

"I think we're the last," said Miriam, following BoBo and Leona through the door.

"Great, then we're off!" Right before Jacey headed outside, she turned and gave Ashley a thumbs-up.

Ashley, who was standing at the back of the lobby, returned the sign, then left the inn by the rear door. Max was waiting for her out on the terrace. They linked hands, and after giving the vans sufficient time to leave, they walked to his car and drove to his boat.

# *Eight*

*Serendipity* lay at anchor in a cove up the coast from the inn. Water lapped quietly against the hull, and the ocean was a lulling undertone beneath it.

Ashley and Max sat at a table on the aft deck, having dinner. In the center of the table a candle's golden flame flickered, protected from the night's breeze by a glass chimney.

The sky around them was a breathtaking black velvet studded with stars, but Max had no eyes for anything but Ashley. She was idly stabbing her baked potato with a fork.

He sat back in his chair and took a sip of wine. "Did Jacey tell you where she was taking everyone tonight?"

"No."

"Do you have a guess as to where they all might be?"

"No."

"Is there something wrong with your baked potato?"

"No."

He smiled. "Ashley, is there something in particular bothering you?"

"No."

"Could you do something for me?"

"No." Her head snapped up as his question registered. "I mean, yes."

"Would you please put your fork down and talk to me?"

"Sure," she said, dropping the utensil. "What would you like to talk about?"

"I'd like to know what you've been thinking about so hard ever since we came on board tonight."

"Cabo San Lucas," she said, as usual speaking before she considered the possibility of censoring herself.

He looked at her in surprise. "Why were you thinking about Cabo?"

She held up her glass and studied the burgundy color of the wine, attempting not to look at him. But in his slim-fitting navy slacks and an open-necked midnight-blue polo shirt that left his muscled forearms bare, he compelled her attention and her desire. "I was just wondering what was there for you. I mean, what is it about the place that would make you want to go down there?"

"That's easy. I've spent some of the greatest fishing days of my life down there."

"You like to fish?"

"It's one of my many passions. Many," he said again, his expression subtly changing as he gazed at her.

She cleared her throat against its sudden dryness. She was very familiar with his passion for her, but she wasn't happy to know that he had others. "Exactly how many passions do you have? Many would seem to imply a large, indefinite number. For instance, are we talking about as many stars as there are in the heavens, or can we narrow it down a bit and limit the number to say, oh"—she shrugged—"the Milky Way Galaxy?"

He hadn't been honest with her, he thought. Just recently he had come to the conclusion that the things he had viewed as his passions before he had met her had turned out to be merely hobbies. Knowing Ashley, loving Ashley, had taught him the true meaning of the word passion. She was his one and only now.

"What is it you want to know?" he asked gently.

"Nothing terribly specific. Well, maybe just a little specific. That is, it occurs to me that I don't know a lot about you other than the fact that you once worked on Wall Street, now own an inn, and don't want a serious relationship. I'm mildly curious about each of those things." She paused and rubbed her temple. "Okay, okay, if you really want to know the absolute, bottom-line truth, I'm wild to know all the whys and the wherefores. *Everything.*" It was only fair. At the moment he was consuming every minute of her waking hours, and she was desperate to figure out why.

"Okay, I'll start with the first thing you know about me. I worked on Wall Street—"

"Mother said you didn't just work there. That you were one of the big kahunas there."

He grinned. "Your mother actually used the word *kahuna*, did she?"

"No, that was my word. Mother has probably never even heard of the word. She did say, though, that you were very *big* there and ruled supreme along with Damien and others."

He chuckled. "Let's just say that I was very good at what I did. And in a relatively short period of time, I managed to amass enough money to last me my entire life."

Picking up a roll, she began to absently pinch off pieces from it. "That's quite a feat. You should be very proud of yourself."

"I don't know that I can take credit for something that came so naturally to me."

"Do you miss it at all?"

"Not really. Besides, I still dabble."

"Dabble." She repeated the word thoughtfully, trying to remember something. "Oh, yes. The computers and fax in your office."

"Right."

"So what made you leave a profession that you were so successful at?"

"Because I had done it. I had lived that so called life-on-the-fast-track, worked those ungodly hours, and made vaults full of money. But the thought of spending the rest of my life doing the same thing over and over again got to me, so I decided to go out and discover what else there was to do."

She dropped the roll and sat forward, her eyes sparkling with understanding. "And so you came out here and bought the inn."

He smiled at her. "I wanted to settle somewhere that was the exact opposite of the life I had left behind. I also wanted a small business that wouldn't require a lot of my attention. I wanted to be able to sleep late if I wanted, and to have the freedom to be able to go somewhere new and interesting at a moment's notice, and stay as long as I wanted."

"I guess that's why you named your boat *Serendipity*. Because you never know what new and wonderful things you'll find around the next corner."

His smile broadened. "That's exactly right. Because you never know." He had looked around one night and unexpectedly discovered *her*. Now he had no further plans to set out and find anything new and wonderful unless she was by his side.

"Sometimes I think I drift for the same reason. No one thing has ever been able to hold my interest for long."

His smile faded. "You conquer one thing and then move on to the next."

She laughed. "I wouldn't exactly say I *conquer* things. I've never been that good at anything. As a kid, I couldn't even make a decent mud pie."

"How long did you try?"

"To make a mud pie?" At his nod she grinned. "About six minutes. Looking back, I think the problem was that I got too much water in my little mud reservoir, which, as I recall, was Mother's begonia bed, but at any rate I eventually, after six minutes, decided it would be much more fun to run through the sprinklers."

He chuckled. "Maybe the reason you've never been too good at any one thing is because you haven't stayed long enough to really apply your-self."

"That's what Jacey says. But it doesn't matter." Or at least it hadn't mattered until she had met him. And now she was unsettled and worried, not only about her drifting habit, but also about the idea of waking up one morning to find that he had taken off to Cabo San Lucas or other, equally faraway places.

"And maybe the reason you keep drifting from thing to thing," he said, continuing, "is because you haven't found anything that's worth staying for."

Many people over the years had tried their hand at pop psychology with her. She had taken their efforts about as seriously as she would a party game. No matter what her friends and family thought to the contrary, she had always had a handle on herself and her life. But not any longer.

"More wine?"

"No, thank you."

"Have you had enough to eat?"

She glanced down at her plate and saw that she had barely touched her food. "Mercy, what hap-pened to my potato? It looks like a teeny-tiny army tramped through it."

"A fork can also make a potato look that way."

"Oh." She speared a shrimp, gazed at it for a moment, then put it back down. "Okay, you've told me about one and two. What about three?"

"Three?"

"The third thing I know about you. That you don't want a serious relationship. Is there some particular reason? I mean, have you been badly hurt by a woman at some point? I can't imagine any woman hurting you, though I guess those things can happen. . . ."

This was going to be tricky. His main objective was to keep her with him, not send her skittering away in fright. "No, I haven't been hurt. I suppose it's been more a matter of lifestyle. Just like you."

"Excuse me?"

"By your own admission, you drift. You laid all your cards on the table with me right up front and made sure I understood you wouldn't be around long."

She chewed on her bottom lip. It had seemed like a good idea at the time. "That wasn't *exactly* what I said."

"No, what you actually said was that you didn't plan to drift away anytime soon, because of your mother and her guests. But I don't imagine they're going to stay long, do you?"

She frowned. He never agreed with her. Why should she agree with him? "I thought we were talking about you."

"We are. I just was trying to show you that we're alike in some ways. I like the life I've created for myself, but I'm not sure there are too many women out there who would."

Her annoyance quickly changed back to curiosity. "Why on earth wouldn't they?"

"There are a lot of people who are very rigid in their thinking. You've said it yourself. I'm young to be retired. People tend to raise eyebrows at healthy men who don't have a conventional nine-to-five job and don't appear to work in any other way."

"That's nonsense."

"I agree, but not everyone does. And so I avoid the possibility that I might get serious about anyone and that some woman might want to tie me down, thereby circumventing the problem before it happens."

He watched her as she picked up the fork and began stabbing her potato once more. Had he said too much? Had he said enough? Lord help him, he wasn't used to walking on eggshells. What he really wanted to do was grab her and tell her flat-out that there was no way she was ever going to leave him. Unfortunately he knew he couldn't do that. But what he could do was use every devious method he could think of to ensure that in the end she would be his and only his.

"You know, I don't think I'm very hungry," she said, pushing back from the table and standing. She started to clear the table, stacking everything on a tray.

"You look tired," he said.

She was astonished at his comment, but then she realized she really did feel tired. "What time is it?"

"Nine-thirty."

"I guess we should head back soon." She lifted the now-full tray.

"Not yet." He blew out the candle, then stood and took the tray from her. "Jacey promised to keep everyone occupied well into the night."

"But—"

"Go on down to the bedroom, and I'll be there as soon as I take the dishes to the galley."

Her heartbeat accelerated. So they were going to make love again. Amazingly she was ready, willing, and even eager. On her dying day, she would remember Max Hayden and marvel over the extraordinary way he had made her feel. On her dying day she would wonder where he was and who he was with. And wonder why she was wondering.

With a nod she made her way to the cabin. There, she undressed, pulled down the covers, and climbed into bed. He soon joined her, but without taking off his clothes first, only his shoes, much to her surprise.

"Why didn't you get undressed?" she asked, confused.

He pulled her to him until her head was resting in the crook of his shoulder and her arm lay over his chest. "I'd like for us to sleep for a while if you don't mind."

"*Sleep?*" She found that she did mind. Very much. There it was—evidence that she was an utterly hopeless wanton. "Don't you want me?"

He chuckled. "So much so that I kept on my clothes to reduce the temptation. Although to be perfectly honest, I don't think it reduced it much at all. The sight of you as you are now would tempt a statue to come alive."

"Then why?"

He combed his fingers lightly through her silky hair. "Because you're tired and could use a few hours of uninterrupted sleep, and I wouldn't mind it myself."

"Then you're tired too?" She tilted her head back to look at his face.

He smiled. "Yes."

"Wouldn't you rather go back to the inn? You could go to your own room and—"

"I'd rather be with you here, alone, holding you. Now close your eyes, and whatever you do, be still."

He wanted to sleep with her without making love to her. She thought about that and felt a warm glow.

She had fallen asleep with him this morning, but not before they had made love. In the past twenty-four hours they had done some mind-blowingly outrageous things to each other that in anyone's book would certainly be described as intimate.

Now they were falling asleep together, not because of any sexual reason, but because they would simply rather be together than apart. She was struck by what an incredibly intimate thing they were doing.

He continued to gently stroke her hair. Her eyelids grew heavy, then closed, and she slept. Happy.

Ashley wasn't in bed with him. The realization came to Max as soon as he awoke. He turned on the light and looked at his watch. Three A.M. Quickly he stood and went in search for her.

He found her in the galley, standing by the stove, looking incredibly sexy in one of his shirts, her long legs and feet bare, her hair a disheveled mass of uncombed waves around her face. And the warm smile she gave him when she glanced around and saw him made his heart turn over.

"Hi. I hope you don't mind my using your galley, but I woke up hungry."

He crossed to her, came up behind her, and wrapped his arms around her waist. "Why didn't you wake me up?" He pushed her hair to one side so he could nuzzle his lips against her neck. "I would have been glad to make you anything you wanted."

"There was no need for that. I enjoy cooking, though I don't have a lot of opportunity to unless I'm home. But don't worry. I'm cooking enough for both of us. I was hoping you'd wake up in time to eat with me." If he hadn't, she might have gone and wakened him. It hadn't been that long since she had left the bedroom, but she had already begun to long for his company.

She was really going to have to do something about herself, she reflected. But offhand, she couldn't think of a thing that would be an antidote against Max.

He gazed over her shoulder at the stove and saw two skillets. Whisked eggs were in one, simmering butter in the other. "What are you making?"

"Omelets."

"It looks like a big yellow pancake."

"I know," she said, giggling. "But in a minute it's going to look like an omelet. I found cheese and mushrooms for the filling. I was surprised at the fresh foods I found."

"The galley was just restocked for the trip."

"Oh, yes," she murmured, frowning at the concoction in the skillet. "Cabo San Lucas. Have you been able to repair the problem you were having with the boat's motor?"

"Not yet."

Her frown lessened. "So you'll be around for a little while longer?"

"Definitely." There had been something odd in her voice when she had asked her questions. He straightened away from her, then turned and leaned back against the counter so he could see her expression.

She lifted both skillets, and with a quick movement of her wrist she flipped the eggs, raw side down, into the second skillet and placed it on the fire.

"I've never seen an omelet cooked in two pans before," he said, fascinated.

"I couldn't find a spatula—thus the two pans."

He opened a drawer, poked around in it, closed it. Opened a second drawer and, after a minute, produced a spatula.

She glanced at the utensil without interest. "Don't worry about it. This is working fine. And now I can start on your omelet." She reached for a bowl and emptied the three whisked eggs in it into the first skillet.

"Where do you want to eat?" he asked, reaching for two plates. "Do you want to go back up on deck?"

She considered his question. "Are you up for a little decadence?"

He saw her mischievous smile, and his eyes began to twinkle. "Absolutely."

"Then let's eat in bed."

They ate in bed and, when they were finished, looked at each other and realized they were still hungry. For each other. With an astounding knowledge of her body, he stroked, kissed, probed, and gently bit, taking her to the edge of madness. Then she mounted him and proceeded to drive him straight over the edge of that madness.

Exhausted by their lovemaking, they finally fell asleep. When they woke again, it was nine in the morning.

"Keep your fingers crossed," Ashley whispered to Max as they climbed the steps to the back terrace. "Maybe Mother and Leona will still be down at the courts."

"Or maybe," he said, not bothering to whisper, "they'll be sitting on the terrace, waiting for us, with shotguns across their laps."

"That's not funny," she hissed, reaching the terrace and peering around the corner. Much to her relief, the only person she saw was Jacey.

Jacey lifted her arm and waved. "Good morning. Come join me for breakfast."

They crossed the terrace and settled themselves at her table. "Where is everyone?" Ashley asked.

"If you mean *the mothers*, they're still in their rooms, nursing giant-sized hangovers."

Ashley almost fell out of her chair. "*My* mother has a hangover? And Leona too?"

Jacey gaily nodded her head. "And everyone else who went with me."

"Way to go," Max said admiringly.

"Thank you."

"Have you checked on them?" Ashley asked. "Are they all right? Do they need a doctor?"

"I checked on everyone, and they all have everything they need. They don't need a doctor, just some time for their systems to forgive them. You'll probably see the first of them start straggling down in an hour or so."

Ashley studied her friend, who as usual looked beautiful and unruffled. "You don't look as if you're suffering any ill effects."

"Are you kidding? I was too busy keeping an eye on all of them to drink."

Max stretched his long legs out in front of him. "Okay, I'm dying of curiosity. Where did you take them?"

"To a biker bar up the coast that one of your bellhops knew about. It was—"

"Excuse me," Ashley said, leaning forward and eyeing her friend intently, "but I just have to interrupt you to make sure that I heard you correctly. Did you say *biker* bar? Bike, as in Harley Davidson? Bikers, as in Hell's Angels?"

"That's what I said."

Ashley's brow crinkled. "I need a Coke."

"I can't tell you how much fun everyone had. It was a first for all of us."

"I can't even begin to imagine any of those people in a biker bar, much less my mother. What happened?"

"When we first arrived, the group was a little stiff. They sat down and didn't so much as twitch a muscle for fear of calling attention to themselves."

"And I suppose they were already the center of the attention," Max said.

"The bikers were riveted by all of us. They

couldn't figure out, what we were doing there. Anyway, I asked the bartender what the drink of the house was, and he said it was a tequila shooter, so I ordered doubles for everyone."

Ashley's eyes widened. "What was in the drink?"

"Don't ask. But after only one, the group got pretty loose. After two, they were mingling among the bikers as if they were at some sort of social reception. And after three, they were treating the bikers like long-lost friends."

Max broke out laughing. "That must have been a sight to see."

"It was truly a remarkable evening in more ways than one," Jacey said. "My only regret is that I didn't have the foresight to bring along a video camera."

"What about the bikers?" Ashley asked. "Were they in the market for new friends?"

"They were wonderful. They didn't even blink when Jean Marc suddenly began to draw sketches of clothes on the paper napkins. By the way, don't be surprised if his next collection features lots of black leather and studs."

Ashley clapped her hands with glee. "Haute couture meets California bikers. I love it."

Jacey chuckled. "Wait, there's more. Two of the bikers made gifts of their leather jackets to Miriam and Leona, and the mothers walked out of the bar on cloud nine, proudly wearing their jackets with the biker's club insignia on the back." Ashley's mouth dropped open. Jacey nodded. "Sort of boggles the mind, doesn't it?"

"Did their hair get messed up?" Max asked.

"Just a little when the guys took everyone for a ride on the back of their bikes."

Ashley shook her head in amazement. "Maybe I should get the recipe for that drink. It might solve all my problems where this wedding is concerned."

"I don't think so," Jacey said. "The mothers wrote down everyone's name and address and promised them all an invitation to the big event."

Ashley groaned.

"Did you get everyone home in one piece?" Max asked Jacey.

"Yes. We had only one close call. Pierre got into a heated argument over the best way to cook a soufflé with a biker who was so big, he looked like a recently uprooted redwood who had gone AWOL from the Redwood National Forest. They almost came to blows, but Greta stepped in and saved Pierre from becoming minced meat. At which point, Pierre declared his love for his magnificent Greta to all and sundry, then retired to the tiny kitchen of the bar and cooked hamburgers for everyone."

Ashley's eyes were alight with glee. "I wish I'd been there."

Max reached over and took her hand. "I'm glad you were with me."

Ashley smiled at him. "Now that you mention it, we had a mildly good time ourselves."

"Excuse me? Mildly?"

Jacey looked from Ashley to Max. "Did I mention breakfast? I'm about to have mine. Would you like to join me?"

"Yes," Ashley said definitely. "I want a Coke."

"Excuse me, Miss Whitfield," said one of the

bellboys, coming up beside her. "Our gardener would like to thank you for your help and suggestions, and he said if you have time today, he'd like to talk to you. He's working down by the tennis courts this morning."

"Tell him I'd be glad to talk to him, and I'll come down in a few minutes. And would you please send a waiter out?"

"What's that all about?" Max asked when the bellboy had left.

She shrugged. "Nothing much. I didn't think the rhododendrons were looking too well, so I bought a few things and had them sent to the gardener. I was hoping he wouldn't mind. I'm not an expert by any means, but I know a few tricks."

"Ashley has a very green thumb," Jacey told Max. "She can make anything take root."

Max turned to Ashley, a thoughtful expression on his face. "Rooted things don't drift."

What an odd thing to have occurred to him, she reflected, deliberately looking away from him toward the shimmering ocean. But he was right. It was too bad she couldn't make herself take root.

# Nine

After a friendly chat with the gardener that involved their mutual love of flowers, Ashley went upstairs and took a shower. She half expected Max to join her. She *wanted* him to join her, and when he didn't, she was disappointed. She quickly dressed in shorts and a T-shirt with GRACELAND written in sequins and fashioned as musical notes across its front, then made her way along the balcony to his room. He wasn't there.

Gnawing on her bottom lip, she tried to cope with a fresh wash of disappointment, but she told herself she was being silly. She couldn't expect him to be at her side every moment of the day and night.

And the fact that she wanted him to be was neither sensible, nor intelligent . . . nor sane.

She headed downstairs with the notion of taking a long, solitary walk on the beach. Afterward she would talk to her mother and Leona. There had to be something she could say to them, something she hadn't thought of yet, that would make them finally understand she wasn't going to marry Roger. She just wished she knew what that something was.

When she reached the lobby, she discovered, much to her surprise, that it was once again serene and peaceful. She strolled over to Marge, who was at her post at the reception desk.

"Good morning, Marge. Where is everyone?"

Marge smiled. "By everyone, do you mean the wedding planners?"

Ashley chuckled. "They're the ones. Doesn't make sense that I would actually be seeking them out, does it? I suppose the more prudent course of action would be to run for my life."

Marge chuckled. "They're actually a very nice group. A little strange and excitable at times, but the staff is enjoying them."

"Well, I'm glad about that. I'd hate for them to be putting any of you out."

"Not at all. They're bringing a little glamour and excitement into our lives. And, to answer your question, they're all in the sitting room. I think they're discussing your wedding gown."

Ashley rolled her eyes. "Wonderful." She started off, but then came to a sudden stop and looked back at Marge. "You wouldn't happen to know where Max is, would you?"

"He's in there with them."

"He's in there *with*—Thanks, Marge."

Alarm propelled Ashley toward the sitting room. Max had said he wouldn't tell her mother and the others about their affair, but she didn't know how much patience he had. True he had helped her mother and Leona with the logistics of where the people they had brought in could set up, and he had smoothed things over between Greta and Pierre, but that had been for the sake of his inn and the normal people who were staying there.

Talk of the wedding easily angered him. He had said a wedding between her and Roger would be a catastrophic accident. As many times as she had tried to explain to him that there wasn't going to be a wedding, he couldn't seem to be rational about the subject. Without meaning to, he might blurt out the news of their affair. And then she would have to administer CPR to her mother and Leona, and everything would be a big mess, and . . .

She halted in the doorway of the sitting room. To her amazement and dismay, it had been transformed into a fashion atelier. Sketches were propped on every available surface, and several traveling trunks were opened, with yards of material and trimmings spilling from their drawers and draped all over.

Jean Marc stood in the center, presiding. Two assistants scurried to do his bidding, dutifully holding up this sketch or that trimming. The mothers were seated on the couch, oohing and ahhing over his every idea and suggestion. BoBo was in a nearby armchair, smiling approvingly and taking notes. Next to her, Sybella fondled her crystals and hummed. Jacey was perched on the arm of another chair, one long leg idly swinging back and forth.

And on the floor, at the feet of her mother and Leona, Max sat.

Jean Marc was the first of the group to see her. "Excellent! Here's the bride herself. Now we can really get down to business."

Leona patted the space between herself and Miriam. "Come sit between us, darling. Jean Marc has come up with the most exciting things. We're all practically drooling."

Her gaze went to Max. He was smiling at her, but his expression was absolutely unreadable.

"I can't. I was just on my way down to the beach for a walk."

A chorus of "No!" and "You can't!" was immediately raised.

Max's voice rose above the din. "You can take your walk later, but for now, come join us. We really need your input."

*We?* Had he really just said *we?* Ashley blinked and looked at Max again. Maybe the same group of outer-space aliens that lived inside computers had possessed his body overnight. It was the only explanation she could come up with. Eyeing him warily, she threaded her way around the assistants and trunks, circled Max, and dropped down between her mother and Leona.

Jean Marc rubbed his hands together. "Here's what we're thinking, Ashley. Classical, white, maybe silk taffeta, perhaps with a draped, off-the-shoulder neckline and, of course, the pièce de résistance, a dramatic, seven-or eight-foot train." He pointed to one of his assistants. "Hold up the sketch for her."

"No," Ashley said, without bothering to glance at the sketch.

"Ashley's right," Max said. "White would be totally wrong for her."

She tensed. Here it came. He was about to say their torrid affair automatically eliminated her from wearing white.

Max screwed his face into an expression that foretold an important, yet slightly painful comment. "Ashley's skin is a trifle sallowish."

Ashley sat forward and stared down at him. *"Sallowish?"*

He nodded. "Your skin has a slight yellowish cast to it."

"My skin is golden-beige. *Golden*, Max, not yellow."

Much to her chagrin, each mother took an arm of hers and inspected her skin for themselves.

"You know, darling, I think Max is right."

Leona nodded. "Definitely."

She jerked her arms free, folded them under her breasts, and sat back, feeling maligned. Max had been over every inch of her skin, lavishing attention on it in every way possible, and had never before expressed discontent with its color.

"I'm glad you mentioned the yellow in her skin, Max," Jean Marc said, eyeing his array of fabrics. "And since that's the case, I think something with a warm undertone that would play down the yellow in her skin is definitely called for."

"What about a candlelight satin?" Jacey said.

Ashley threw a glaring look at her friend. *"Et tu, Brute?"*

Lights of humor danced in Jacey's eyes. "I'm only

trying to be helpful. We don't want you to look jaundiced on your wedding day, now do we?"

Max rubbed his hand from Ashley's ankle to her knee and back again. To anyone else, it would undoubtedly seem a casually comforting gesture. But fire streaked where he touched. She was tempted to kick him.

"Jacey's right, Ashley," he said. "All we're trying to do is to make sure your wedding is absolutely perfect and everything you would want it to be."

Her mother beamed at him. "I don't know what we would do without you, Max."

"It's my pleasure, Miriam."

"I'm going to scream" Ashley said to no one in particular.

He tenderly patted her leg, creating more fire. "Just hang in here with us a little longer. We're making real progress. Now, Jean Marc, about the design. Classical is definitely the right approach. But nothing too low either in the front or back. Nothing too tight either. I have always felt very strongly that on a bride's wedding day, she should look pure and virginal. Or at least as pure and virginal as she can manage."

Leona touched his shoulder in approval. "I couldn't agree more."

The scream Ashley had mentioned began to rise in her throat. Then she felt Max's hand drift down to her bare toes and commence stroking each one individually. It had a surprisingly erotic effect on her. Anger, eroticism, bewilderment. What next? she wondered.

"Perhaps a princess-style waist," Max said. "It would help minimize the width of her hips."

The scream rose and became strangled in her throat. "What in the hell do you mean, the width of my hips? I don't have big hips. I've never had big hips. Mother, tell him."

"Of course you don't, darling. You have a perfectly lovely figure. It's just that we want to make sure that all your attributes are emphasized and the few flaws you do have are deemphasized."

Deep in thought, Jean Marc put a finger to his temple. "An embroidery of gold silk threads would help give an added warmth to the fabric, plus we can sprinkle stones over the entire gown."

"Pearls," Max said decisively. "Pearls have a beautiful luminescence about them. I think their luster would help her sallowness problem a great deal."

"You're right," Miriam said.

He slid his hand around to the back of Ashley's calf and lightly massaged it. Warmth spread in all directions through her body. She glanced around the room and saw that no one was paying any attention to what he was doing to her. In fact, now that she took a good look at all of them, she decided there was an excellent possibility that they could all be aliens come down to earth expressly to torment her. And Max was their leader.

"Filling the church with candles would also help," Jacey said.

Max nodded. "I've always thought that candles could cast an illusion of beauty over any woman, no matter how sallow her complexion or how imperfect her features."

"That's it!" Ashley stood. "I'm leaving. You people seem to have the situation well in hand, though I feel compelled to point out one more time that there's not going to be a wedding, and therefore, you are all wasting your time. Hugely."

Miriam and Leona made well-mannered sounds of distress. But Max watched her go with a small smile on his face.

"Don't worry about a thing," he said, rising to his feet. "I'll go talk to her."

"Thank you so much, Max," Miriam said. "I'm at a loss as to why she's behaving like this. I had thought that by now she would have been reassured about her prewedding jitters—"

Leona clucked. "And we haven't even gotten to poor Pierre yet. He's been baking all morning."

"Not to mention the invitations," BoBo said. "We have those to choose yet. I plan to recommend velum with fourteen-karat gold embossing."

Sybella whipped out her laptop computer and began to furiously punch keys.

"I'll see what I can do," Max said, and looked at Jacey. She winked at him.

He caught up with Ashley as she was heading out the door to the terrace. He snaked his hand around her wrist and brought her to an abrupt halt. "Where are you going?"

Her green eyes sparkled with anger as she swung around and glared at him. "I'm going down to the beach, and I'm hoping, I'm *really* hoping, that I don't run into any aliens down there."

"Aliens, Ashley?"

"You know exactly what I mean, and don't pretend that you don't. You've done a complete turn-around on this wedding. First you were dead set against it, and now you're *helping*, for heaven sakes! And for your information, I don't have a sallow tone in my skin, and my hips are not big."

"All I said was that a princess style would help minimize the width of your hips. I didn't actually say they were big."

"Oh, *please.* From the way you and everyone were talking, I wouldn't have been surprised if you'd decided to order a camouflage tent and just drape it over me."

Barely able to keep from laughing, he threw a quick look around, then pulled her toward the potted palm and the concealed doorway. Once inside the luggage-holding room, he backed her up against a hanging garment bag. "Now, Ashley, you're overwrought. What's wrong? You had your morning Coke, didn't you?"

Her teeth snapped together. "My morning Coke has nothing to do with this. It isn't me who's changed. What did you do? Take a helpful pill or something?"

"I think it must have been a passion pill." He leaned against her and kissed the side of her neck. "I want you again."

She pushed against his chest. "Damn you, Max—"

His mouth came down on hers, hard and hungry. Her body responded, coming instantly to life, even while her mind resisted. The pressure she was exerting against his chest lessened as his tongue delved deeply into her mouth and his hand slipped beneath her T-shirt and bra to close around her breast.

She folded her hands into fists, angry that he knew exactly where to touch her and how to kiss her to make her soften and melt. It wasn't fair, her mind told her. But her body countered with a "who cares?" attitude. He made her burn with scintillating pleasure.

"Stop it, Max," she murmured, the words muffled against his lips. Then her arms slid around his neck.

He didn't take his hand from her breast, but he eased his mouth from hers just enough so that he could speak. "You're asking the impossible. Kissing you is a basic need." His fingers flicked back and forth across her nipple, causing her to gasp. "You can't want me to stop. Tell me you don't."

She tried desperately to hold on to her rapidly diminishing thinking processes. "I don't. I mean . . ." Heat was radiating out from her nipple to every part of her body. "I, uh, don't want you to stop, but—"

He tightened his hold on her and positioned her so that she could feel his hardened desire against her pelvis.

"But what?" he muttered huskily.

Her head fell back against the garment bag, and she stared up into the fires that burned in the depths of his blue eyes. "But how can you help plan my wedding to another man one minute and kiss me the next?"

He unzipped her shorts and stripped them off her. He did the same with her panties, then unzipped his own pants. "Your mother and the others are determined to plan the wedding. Right?"

He cupped the soft mounds of her bottom, lifted her, wrapped her legs around his waist, and entered her. Instantly she was enveloped by heat. She might have nodded; she was sure she didn't answer.

"I decided to help expedite it." He began to slowly stroke in and out of her, filling her, withdrawing, then filling her again. "At least this way, when you and Roger get married," he said huskily, "you'll have a beautiful, well-planned wedding."

"But I'm not—"

His stroking intensified, became faster, more powerful, until he was pounding into her. Cushioned by the soft garment bag, she strained to take him deeper into her. She cried out, uncaring if anybody heard. She clung to him, equally uncaring that only a moment ago she'd been angry with him. Her mind became hazy, leaving nothing but feeling, incendiary passion, and, ultimately, an ecstasy that defied description.

Ashley slumped against him, the curls at her forehead dampened and plastered against her skin. He held her tightly to him, the back of his shirt soaked with sweat.

He couldn't talk. Even knowing how much he loved her, he had been shaken by the depth and power of his passion for her. It seemed incomprehensible to him that she didn't return his love, that she still planned to drift away from him. Their need for each other was so basic, so fundamental, so absolutely essential. Why couldn't she see things as plainly as he did?

As much as he hated it, he was going to have to continue with his plan. And pray.

A light knock sounded at the door, and they heard Jacey's voice.

"I'm sorry to bother you two, but the mothers are getting restless. The florist has arrived, and Pierre is anxious for you to sample the cakes."

"Stall them for ten minutes," he said.

"You got it."

Gently he pushed Ashley's head from his shoulder so that it fell back against the garment bag, then he stroked her hair from her face. "We need to sneak upstairs and wash up. And I need to change shirts."

"You know what we really need to do, don't you?" she asked. Her humor had returned, though she was still trying to catch her breath.

"What?"

"We need to stop coming into this luggage-holding room."

He chuckled. "I'm up for exploring other places if you are."

Fifteen minutes later Ashley came back downstairs, washed, refreshed, and wearing a T-shirt that was emblazoned with a big sunflower and KANSAS across its front. She still tingled from head to foot from Max's lovemaking. He had said something to her at the start of it, but for the life of her she couldn't remember what it had been. And it really didn't matter. Their time in the luggage-holding room had completely restored her good spirits.

Max met her at the bottom of the steps, and after a rapid survey of the lobby, planted a quick, hard kiss on her lips.

She smiled up at him, thinking how much she loved his kisses. She was not only good at sex, she thought, pleased, she was also good at kissing. She stood on tiptoes to kiss him back, but much to her disappointment, he took her hand and began walking.

"They're waiting for you in the dining room. This isn't a peak meal time, and I've allowed Pierre to set up a table at one end of the room with the cakes he wants you to taste."

She was going to have difficulty tasting cakes, she thought, when all she could taste was him.

"I told you I would deliver her," Max said when they entered the dining room.

Pierre excitedly clapped his hands together. "Ziz good, ziz good! Come. We are to begin first of all with zee cakes. Zen we will move on, as one, to what will be served at zee dinner. But for zee present minute, sample. Taste. You will adore."

Her mother, Leona, Jacey, and BoBo already had plates in hand, and were taking bites of the different cakes that were spread out over the table.

"Darling, you must try the white-chocolate mousse cake. It is divine."

Leona shook her head. "I'm not sure I agree, Miriam. I've already formed a partiality for the Italian cream. Ashley, Pierre says you can have your choice of fillings. For instance, there's vanilla with brandy, lemon, almond, chocolate crème de cacao, raspberry with crème de cassis, plus several others he can tell you about. And of course the whole cake will be covered with whipped-cream frosting."

She saw Max pick up a plate, and suddenly realized she was hungry. Maybe she'd have a bite or two herself. She reached for a plate.

"How many layers do you think we'll need?" Miriam asked Pierre.

"Many, many. It must be impressive, important, of great consequence." The little man assessed the height of the table, then lifted his gaze upward. "Zee cake, in total measurement with zee table, must be at least ten feet."

"Ummm." Jacey smacked her lips. "This yellow cake with the apricot—Grand Marnier filling is absolutely heavenly."

Pierre's chest puffed out. "I know, I know. I am a god in zee kitchen."

"It all tastes good to me," Ashley said, speaking the truth, for the moment forgetting the reason why she was eating the cake in the first place.

"Ashley's right," Max said, "but I have to say my favorite cake isn't represented here."

Pierre's expression turned to alarm. "What could zat be?"

"German chocolate."

Pierre relaxed. "Zat is usually made for zee groom's cake, and is for zee groom to decide. You understand?"

Max nodded. "Yes, of course."

Max, a groom, waiting at the altar as the woman he was about to marry came toward him. The image had Ashley disregarding the cakes. No matter what he said now, there was a good chance that one day he might fall in love and marry. She felt a peculiar pain in her heart. But, she told herself sternly, she had no right to hurt simply because he might someday marry. The woman, whoever she would be, would no doubt be all wrong for him, but what business was it of hers? After all, she was having only a passionate attachment of limited duration with him.

"I do have a question though," Max said. "What were you thinking for the decoration on the cake?"

"That's a good question," Miriam said, turning to Pierre.

He shrugged. "There are many ways to decorate a cake, *madame*. Out of my kitchen, I can beget anything you would prefer. Real flowers are popular zeez days, but if you like better, I can create confection flowers. Or perhaps you would favor figures of some kind. Like angels, for example."

Max swallowed a mouthful of cake and threw a quick glance at Ashley. He couldn't be sure if she was paying attention, but he plunged ahead anyway. "I think you should use real flowers for the decoration and glue pearls onto their petals and stamens. It would not only carry out the theme of the pearls on Ashley's dress, it would be both trend-setting and exquisitely beautiful."

The mouths of both mothers dropped open with admiration.

"Then," he said, continuing, "you could carry the theme out in Ashley's bouquet. Whatever flower or flowers she chooses, you could insert sprays of pearls that could cascade downward along with the flowers and the ribbons."

Ashley stared at him as if he had sprouted horns.

Miriam found her voice first. "That's genius, Max. Pure genius."

"Thank you," he said, his tone modest. "I think the main thing to remember in making our choices . . ."

Had he really said *our* choices? Ashley wondered.

". . . is to keep everything soft, warm, and golden because of Ashley's skin tone."

Her anger began to simmer. Why did he keep harping on her skin tone as if it were some horrid shade of bright yellow?

"For instance, you wouldn't want to give her a bouquet of calla lilies. They're pure white and would defeat what we're trying to do."

*We.* He had said it again, she thought, her ire rising.

"I'm no flower expert, and I understand the florist is still upstairs unpacking, but I think that there must be quite a few cream-colored flowers we could choose from. Like maybe roses or tulips. Perhaps we could even add just a touch of pale gold in some way to the bouquet. The pearls would cast an iridescent sheen onto everything, and if we use plenty of candles in conjunction with the flowers and the pearls, I'm willing to bet not a single person would notice the sallowness of Ashley's skin."

Both mothers went to Max and hugged him.

Jacey broke into applause. "Bravo, Max. Bravo."

BoBo was furiously scribbling everything he had said in a notebook.

And Ashley suddenly remembered what he had said to her in the luggage-holding room as he had been making love to her. He had said he was helping to expedite the wedding plans so that when she and Roger married, she'd have a beautiful, well-planned wedding. She dropped her plate. It landed on the floor with a loud crash and broke.

She stepped over the china pieces and smushed a slice of cake beneath her heel. "Damn you, Max Hayden! I have no idea what you're trying to do, but I want it stopped right now! Do you hear me? This wedding is none of your business, and—"

"Ashley, darling, that's very impolite."

Barely hearing her mother, Ashley stepped closer to Max so she could emphasize each word by poking him in the chest with a stiff finger. "Stop trying to be so damned helpful! Stop telling everyone who'll listen that I have big hips and sallow skin! And stop taking me into the damned luggage-holding room at every opportunity!"

Leona looked at Miriam. "Luggage-holding room?"

"She must be tired," Miriam said.

"And by the way, while I'm on the subject, if you call my skin sallow one more time, I'm going to go to the kitchen, get the biggest butcher knife I can find, and cut out your heart. *You* of *all* people should know my skin is not sallow. You've seen every inch of my skin, every pore, and—"

She fell abruptly silent. Cautiously she looked around her. Jacey was selecting another piece of cake. BoBo and Pierre were staring with fascination at her. The expression on the two mother's faces bordered on shock.

She took a deep breath. "What I actually meant to say was that, since I've been here, I've been wearing the little outfits I bought in the boutique, and, well, Mother, you said it yourself. That one I had on the day Jacey arrived was pretty bare. I didn't actually mean to suggest that Max had seen ever pore. Goodness, no, not even every *inch.* Maybe just a portion here and there, and a very *small* portion, at that. You know, like a shoulder, maybe a little of my neck." She glared at Max, who innocently returned her gaze. She was digging her grave deeper and deeper, and he wasn't going to help her.

*"You little worm! I'm going to kill you!"*

Immensely grateful for the interruption, Ashley glanced around to see who had saved her. It was Greta, marching toward Pierre with a meat cleaver in her hand. A meat cleaver! What a good idea, she thought grimly. Why go after someone with a butcher knife when you could use a meat cleaver?

Max moved to position himself between Greta and Pierre. "What's wrong?"

"That moronic twit threw my sourdough starter down the disposal!"

Pierre stepped out from behind Max, his eyes wide with concern that his adorable Greta was angry. "But, no! I only threw a great lump of library paste down zee sink. I needed to make room in zee refrigeration box for my poached salmon in pink champagne aspic." He threw a glance at Ashley. "Zat is my recommendation to start zee dinner." He kissed his fingers. *"Magnifique!"*

Greta waved the meat cleaver in the air. "You stupid, imbecilic Frenchman! That wasn't library paste. That was the sourdough starter that I make my biscuits from. What's more, it's the original starter that I inherited from my great-great-great-grandfather who came to California for the Gold Rush in forty-nine."

Pierre clapped his hands to his cheeks. "But, *no*! I am desolate zat I did such a thing. My Greta, how can I make it up to you? Tell me, I will move a mountain, swim an ocean, capture for you a star!"

Greta was unmoved. "Come to my kitchen, put your head on my chopping block, and we'll call it even."

"Now, Greta," Max said. "Calm down and think about this. That starter was divided equally among you and your sisters. It will be an easy matter to get some from one of them, and it will still be your great-great-great-grandfather's."

"It won't be the same, Max."

"It will be exactly the same. Don't two of your sisters live in San Francisco? I'll send one of the staff to whichever sister you choose, and we'll have you a fresh batch of starter back here by tonight."

"Well, I don't know—"

"Greta, I explained to you how important this wedding is that we're all planning. Now I really would appreciate your cooperation. . . ."

Something snapped in Ashley, and she was unable to hear anything else Max was saying. Her nerves had stretched to the point that it was impossible for her to stand there one more minute and hear about wedding cakes or flowers or biscuit starters. She was fed up with it all, but most of all she was fed up with Max.

She slipped her hands into the pockets of her shorts and found not only the key to her room but also her car keys. She turned on her heels and walked out.

# Ten

She got lost. Naturally, she thought with grim sarcasm, since she was trying to get *away* from Max instead of *to* him.

When she pulled into the parking lot of the inn, it was close to midnight, and from what she could see, most of the room lights were out. That was good, she told herself, though she hadn't really expected her mother and Leona to be worried about her leaving so abruptly. They were used to her drifting off and getting lost. They knew she always came back. But on further reflection, it did seem to her that Max might have had the decency to be a little concerned about her. Not that she cared.

Lying in his bed, Max heard her as she opened the door to her room and went in. And he said a silent, heartfelt prayer of thanks that she had come back.

It had been agony for him, waiting, wondering

where she was, wondering if she would decide to keep on going, to keep on drifting. Several times he had almost called the police to initiate a search for her, but he knew if they found her, she would be even more furious than she had been when she had left. Besides, he hadn't really believed anyone could find her. Not even him. She didn't travel in straight lines, and she ignored boundaries.

But she was back now. He had another chance.

He wondered if he would have the strength to wait for her to come to him.

She wouldn't go to him, she thought angrily. Why should she? She was still furious with him, and she had every right to be. He had played her as if she were some sort of musical instrument. And like a fool she had cooperated beautifully, allowing him to play whole compositions in her mind and on her body.

He had disturbed her, he had bothered her, he had made her insane. And none of that had changed. He was still affecting her in the very same ways. But though every part of her might be crying out for him, she wouldn't go to him. Never again, she vowed. Never again.

Max rolled over, looked at the clock, and cursed. It would defeat his purpose if he went to her. He wanted her, but for more than just tonight. He wanted her forever, as his wife.

But it was plain. She wasn't going to come.

He had set upon a course that he had hoped

would jolt her into seeing more clearly what was happening. She was used to her mother and the others. By her own admission they weren't saying anything she hadn't heard before. For all practical purposes she was ignoring them.

He had hoped that when he joined them in planning the wedding, she wouldn't be able to ignore him as easily. His intention had been to throw her off balance, make her a little angry, and most of all to make her think. He wanted her to put a stop to the wedding planning before it went any further and to stop drifting. And most of all, to come to see that she loved him.

Lord, he hoped, *prayed*, she loved him.

The last couple of days he had taken a gamble, but he refused to believe he had lost. And he would never give up.

Discounting the way she had kept blundering into him when they had first met, he had been the aggressor in their affair. Now he felt it was psychologically important for her that she come to him. But if she wouldn't, he wasn't too proud to go to her. Still . . .

He thought about his problem for a minute. There was a way he could give her an excuse and make it easier for her to come to him. Unfortunately it would only work if she really wanted to come to him. Another gamble.

He reached for the phone and placed a call to the front desk.

Max's phone was ringing. Ashley frowned. Dammit, why didn't he answer the phone? How could he bear that shrill ring, time and time again, and not want to tear the phone out of the wall? Or at the very least, answer it?

She sat up in bed and stared at her open French doors. Was she the only person in the world who cared whether a phone was answered or not? It was late, she was tired, she couldn't go around answering every Tom, Dick, and Harry's phone. And she certainly didn't want to answer *Max's* phone. She didn't want to go near him or his room.

She flounced out of bed and began to pace. The phone continued to ring. The sound was like a screech to her ears.

Either he wasn't in his room, or he was sound asleep.

She could shut the French doors or put cotton in her ears. Or she could put a pillow over her head. She could even call the front desk and tell them to take a message for Max.

But she knew she wasn't going to do any of those things.

Only moonlight illuminated the dark room, but as her eyes adjusted to the dim light, she could make out Max's form. He was lying on his back, still, asleep.

She hadn't seen him for hours, and now just the sight of him had her heart beating like a drum. And the phone kept ringing.

Unable to tear her gaze from him, she walked slowly around the bed toward the phone. As she grew nearer, she could see him more clearly, the

outline of his arms and legs, his features, his eyes
She halted in her tracks.

His eyes were open, and he was watching her.

Without taking his gaze from hers, he reached
over to the phone, brought the receiver to his ears
and said, "Thanks." Then he hung up.

"You had someone call you?" she asked, completely stunned.

"Yes."

"So that I would come answer it?"

"Yes."

"Why?"

He held out his arms to her.

She felt vulnerable, a completely new sensatio
for her. It was as if he could see through her int
her heart.

And not even she could do that.

To make it worse, she had no defense agains
him. She stood there trembling, as if she were o
the brink of something significant and mayb
even a little dangerous. But she knew that couldr
be. In the short time she had known Max, they ha
made love many times. She wasn't afraid of hir
So why did she feel so vulnerable? She didr
know.

But she did know the answer to at least or
question. She was going to make love to him.

Slowly, hesitantly, she grasped the hem of th
chemise she wore, lifted it over her head, a
tossed it aside. Then she walked to the bed and l
down beside him.

He rolled over on his side toward her, smooth
his hand over her stomach and up to her breas
and whispered her name. She could feel the he

from his body radiating outward to hers, penetrating her pores, inserting itself into her bloodstream.

He kissed and caressed her, enveloping her with his strength, overwhelming her with his attention. Her nipples hardened, the muscles of her belly clenched, her urgency grew. She whimpered and twisted in his arms; her back arched off the bed. "Max . . ."

He positioned himself between her legs and entered her. Her body opened for him as if it were welcoming him home. Intense pleasure burst inside her, and she wrapped her legs around his hips, locking him to her.

"Deeper," she murmured, wanting his entire length, wanting to absorb him completely. "Deeper."

He shuddered and buried himself in her with a hard, strong thrust.

Fires detonated into life all over her. She clung to him, refusing to let him go. He was dominating her with his strength and power, yet she felt as if she were the one in control. Each time his hips pulled back from her, he seemed to hold his breath until he could drive into her again. Only when they were joined as one did he breathe, and she breathed with him, unconsciously adopting the speed and rhythm of his pulse and his breathing rate.

Nothing was new in the way he was making love to her, yet everything was new. The sensations were still incredible, but emotions were being tapped into as well, something she hadn't noticed happening the previous times they'd made love.

Amid the frantic thrusting and undulating,

amid the harsh breathing and sweating flesh amid the urgent cries and pleas, she felt a belonging and a closeness she had never felt before, a safety and tenderness that swelled her heart and made tears swim in her eyes.

Hard, sweet sex combined with heartwarming joy was all-consuming. Her skin, her nerves, the sensitive bud buried deep within the folds of her womanhood, all began to ache unbearably, and her completion came with a force that blacked out everything. Everything, except Max.

She loved him.

Beside her, she heard his deep, even breathing and knew that he had fallen asleep.

She loved him.

Her mind spun with her new discovery, and there was no way she could sleep. Inside her emotions were roiling turbulently, colliding, multiplying, magnifying.

She didn't know how it had happened, or even exactly when. Her preoccupation with the wedding, her mother, and all the others who had flown in had acted as a buffer, keeping her from figuring out exactly what was occurring.

But even if she had known, there was nothing she could have done to stop her love from taking root and growing. Her love was too powerful.

In her mind she had always referred to the sexual encounters as "making love." And now she knew why. She had been making love to him in every sense of the word; it had just taken her a while to catch on to the fact.

In the darkness she smiled. She was happier than she could ever remember being. Love had put bubbles into her bloodstream, making it feel as if champagne were running through her veins. She was intoxicated, elated.

She was scared.

Her smiled slowly faded. Max didn't want a serious relationship. He wanted his lifestyle just as it was, and he had as much as told her that he didn't want anyone or anything to interfere with it.

He didn't love her.

Still, she knew what she had to do.

Max woke late and alone. He didn't like waking alone, and he especially didn't like the fact that he didn't know where Ashley was. Had she left again? Maybe this time for good?

He bolted from the bed and ran down the balcony to her room. He relaxed only when he saw that all her clothes were still in the closet.

Returning to his room, he showered, dressed, and then went downstairs in search of her. "Marge, has Ashley checked out?"

"No. I saw Ashley and her mother earlier."

Satisfied, he went into the dining room. Seating himself at his table, he waited for his usual order of coffee and toast to be brought to him. A waiter poured him a cup of coffee immediately, but the whole-wheat toast was longer in coming.

When the waiter finally brought it to him, it was with an apology. "Sorry, but Greta's not herself today, and consequently everyone in the kitchen is in a tizzy."

Max groaned. "Pierre, right? What's he done now?"

"He's left to go back to New York."

"You're kidding!"

"No. And Greta is in a royal-blue funk. Seems she's missing the little guy."

Max thoughtfully munched on his toast. After Ashley had taken off yesterday, the mothers must have decided to go ahead and choose the cake. It was a practical thing for them to do, but it also made his blood boil. It was a perfect example of what he had been trying to get Ashley to see. The wedding was like a runaway horse, and pretty soon all she was going to be able to do was hang on until it stopped at the altar.

After his breakfast he decided to check with Jean Marc in the sitting room and see if he knew what had happened with Pierre.

No one was in the sitting room. What's more, there were no signs of sketches, traveling trunks, or lengths of material.

He blew out a long breath of air and returned to the reception desk. "Marge, where's Jean Marc?"

"He checked out early this morning and took a limo back to San Francisco."

The hairs on the back of his neck began to prickle. "Who else has checked out?"

"Everyone who was involved with the wedding planning, with the exception of Ashley and her mother."

What in the hell was going on? "And where are they?"

"I believe Mrs. Whitfield went up to her room, and Ashley said she was going down to the beach."

It took him ten heart-stopping minutes to find her. She was behind a sand dune, gazing at the ocean, her arms around her drawn-up legs.

He dropped down beside her and rested one arm on a bent knee. "Marge says everyone's left but you and your mother."

Slowly she turned her head and looked at him. His blue eyes were opaque, making it difficult for her to gauge his mood. "That's right."

"Why did they leave?"

"Jacey took off for Australia to find something new she's never done before, and everyone else left because their job here was finished."

"I see." His hand clenched and unclenched.

"I sent them home."

"*You* sent them home? And they left, just like that, without protest, including Leona?"

She hesitated, unsure about his reaction. But she wanted to tell him everything. "I finally figured out what to say to everyone to make them hear me. Roger and I definitely won't be getting married."

His relief was profound, but short-lived because he was left with another problem. "And when are you leaving?"

That was certainly the $64,000 question, she reflected. And it all depended on him. Would he allow her to put down roots with him as she so desperately wanted? She didn't know. She felt as if her life and happiness were precariously balanced, and it would take only a nudge to send her plummeting.

"When do you want me to leave?"

Her question was a shocker, implying that her departure was up to him. If he had been standing,

he would have had to sit. Since he was uncertai
why she had asked the question, he formed hi
answer carefully. "Suppose I say I don't want yo
ever to leave?"

Her eyes were very green, very serious. "If yo
said that, would you mean it?"

"If I said it, Ashley, I would mean it."

Hope surged, but she proceeded cautiousl
"Okay, then, could you, I mean, do you think yo
would be able to say it now, or maybe sometime i
the future?"

His expression softened. He took her face b
tween his two hands. "It would be the easiest thin
in the world for me to say. I'll show you. Ashley,
don't want you to ever leave me. And do you kno
why?"

Her heart began to warm. "No. Well, that i
maybe. We're terrific together in bed, but we ca
spend the rest of our lives in bed or in the luggag
holding room. At least I don't feel that we can. S
uh, I hope your reason for wanting me to stay
about roots and because . . . and because y
love me."

"Give that girl the jackpot," he said tenderly.
pressed a soft kiss to her lips. "Yes, Ashley, I lo
you. I love you, I love you, I love you." He chuckl
"I've just told you I love you four times, and tha
something I never thought I'd hear myself say
any woman even once."

She smiled, and tears sprang to her eyes. "H
perfect."

He drew a deep, ragged, painful breath. "Not y
Not completely. There are a couple of things I wa
to hear. The first being what you said that fin
convinced everyone to leave."

"I told them I loved you." He looked at her, and she nodded. "It's true. And for Mother, hearing that I love you was enough. She only wanted my happiness; it's all she's ever wanted. And she already likes you tremendously. Besides, I pointed out to her and Leona that this way they could have two weddings." Her tone turned cautious. "One when, and of course *if*, you and I marry, and one when Roger marries. They got very excited over that idea. I should have thought of it sooner. And Sybella says we have perfectly matching astrological charts, and—"

He reached out and covered her mouth with his hand. "Ashley, do you mean it? Are you absolutely sure? Do you really love me?"

She smiled, and he dropped his hand. "With all my heart. I've been a trifle slow about everything, Max, but last night, I finally figured it out. At last I drifted up against something that wouldn't allow me to move on. You. And if you hadn't loved me back, I'm not sure what I would have done with the rest of my life. But one way or the other, my drifting days would have been over."

He shouted with joy, then asked the question he had been bursting to ask. "Ashley, will you marry me?"

*"Yes, oh yes!"* Suddenly her mind took a radical turn, and mischievous lights appeared in her eyes. "What I really meant to say was that it all depends. Do you really think my skin is sallow and my hips are too big? I mean, I'd hate for you to be saddled with a bride who—"

Knowing that no one could see them, he pushed her down to the golden sand. "I've never seen skin as beautiful as yours, Ashley, and your hips fit perfectly into my hands."

He took her slowly, for the first time able to bring his love out into the open and show her how much he loved her. She received that love gladly and returned it tenfold. With their cries of ecstasy mingling with the sound of the ocean, the breeze, and the sea gulls, their love bonded them for all time more surely than any marriage vows ever could.

Much later, arm in arm, they strolled back to the inn. Miriam was on the terrace, seated at a table busily jotting down notes in her burgundy leather organizer. When they climbed the stairs to her, she rose and hugged and kissed each one.

"Darlings, I'm so happy for you both, and I don't want you to worry about one single thing. Your wedding is going to be a magnificent affair!"

Glowing with happiness, Ashley looked up at Max and whispered, "We've already had a magnificent affair."

He leaned down and touched his mouth to her ear, ensuring only she could hear. "And our magnificent affair is going to continue for the rest of our lives."

# THE EDITOR'S CORNER

The coming month brings to mind lions and lambs—not only in terms of the weather but also in terms of our six delightful LOVESWEPTs. In these books you'll find fierce and feisty, warm and gentle characters who add up to a rich and exciting array of folks whose stories of falling in love are enthralling.

Let Joan Elliott Pickart enchant you with her special brand of **NIGHT MAGIC,** LOVESWEPT #534. Tony Murretti knows exactly what he wants when he hires Mercy Sloan to design the grounds of his new home, but he never expected what he gets—a spellbinding redhead who makes him lose control! Tony vowed long ago never to marry, but the wildfire Mercy sparks in his soul soon has him thinking of settling down forever. This book is too good to resist.

Fairy tales can come true, as Jordon Winters learns in award-winning Marcia Evanick's **GRETCHEN AND THE BIG BAD WOLF,** LOVESWEPT #535—but only after he's caught in a snowdrift and gets rescued by what looks like a snow angel in a horse-drawn sleigh. Gretchen Horst is a seductive fantasy made gloriously real . . . until he discovers she's the mayor of the quaint nearby town and is fiercely opposed to his company's plan to build new homes there. Rest assured that there's a happy ending to this delightful romance.

Terry Lawrence's **FOR LOVERS ONLY,** LOVESWEPT #536, will set your senses ablaze. Dave King certainly feels on fire the first time he kisses his sister-in-law Gwen Stickert, but she has always treated him like a friend. When they're called to mediate a family fight at a romantic mountain cottage, Dave decides it's time to raise the stakes—to flirt, tease, and tantalize Gwen until she pleads for his touch. You're sure to find this romance as breathlessly exciting as we do.

Janet Evanovich returns with another one of her highly original and very funny love stories, **NAUGHTY NEIGH-**

**BOR,** LOVESWEPT #537, for which she created the most unlikely couple for her hero and heroine. Pete Streeter is a handsome hellraiser in tight-fitting jeans while Louisa Brannigan is a congressman's aide who likes to play it safe. When these two get entangled in a search for a missing pig, the result is an unbeatable combination of hilarious escapades and steamy romance. Don't miss this fabulous story!

You'll need a box of tissues when you read Peggy Webb's emotionally powerful **TOUCHED BY ANGELS,** LOVESWEPT #538. Jake Townsend doesn't think he'll ever find happiness again—until the day he saves a little girl and she and her mother, Sarah Love, enter his life. Sarah makes him want to believe in second chances, but can her sweet spirit cleanse away the darkness that shadows his soul? Your heart will be touched by this story, which is sure to be a keeper. Bravo, Peggy!

Spice up your reading with **A TASTE OF TEMPTATION** by Lori Copeland, LOVESWEPT #539, and a hero who's Hollywood handsome with a playboy's reputation to match. Taylor McQuaid is the type that Annie Malone has learned only too well never to trust, but she's stuck with being his partner in cooking class. And she soon discovers he'll try anything—in and out of the kitchen—to convince her he's no unreliable hotshot but his own man. An absolutely terrific romance.

On sale this month from FANFARE are four fabulous novels. National bestseller **TEXAS! SAGE** by Sandra Brown is now available in the paperback edition. You won't want to miss this final book in the sizzling TEXAS! trilogy, in which Lucky and Chase's younger sister Sage meets her match in a lean, blue-eyed charmer. Immensely talented Rosanne Bittner creates an unforgettable heroine in **SONG OF THE WOLF.** Young, proud, and beautiful, Medicine Wolf possesses extraordinary healing powers and a unique sensitivity that leads her on an odyssey into a primeval world of wildness, mystery, and passion. A compelling novel by critically acclaimed Diana Silber, **LATE NIGHT DANCING** follows the lives of three friends—sophisticated Los Angeles women who are busy, successful, and on the fast track of romance and sex, because, like women everywhere, they hunger for a man to love. Finally, the ever-popular Virginia Lynn lets her imagination soar across the ocean to England in the historical romance **SUMMER'S KNIGHT**. Heiress Summer St. Clair is stranded penniless on the streets of London, but her terrifying ordeal soon turns to passionate adventure when she catches the glittering eyes of the daring Highland rogue Jamie Cameron.

Also on sale this month in the Doubleday hardcover edition (and in paperback from FANFARE in May) is **LADY HELLFIRE** by Suzanne Robinson, a lush, dramatic, and poignant historical romance. Alexis de Granville, Marquess of Richfield, is a cold-blooded rogue whose dark secrets have hardened his heart to love—until he melts at the fiery touch of Kate Grey's sensual embrace. Still, he believes himself tainted by his tragic—and possibly violent—past and resists her sweet temptation. Tormented by unfulfilled desires, Alexis and Kate must face a shadowy evil before they can surrender to the deepest pleasures of love. . . .

Happy reading!

With warmest wishes,

*Nita Taublib*

Nita Taublib
Associate Publisher/LOVESWEPT
Publishing Associate/FANFARE

**Don't miss these fabulous Bantam Fanfare titles on sale in FEBRUARY.**

## TEXAS! SAGE
*by Sandra Brown*

## SONG OF THE WOLF
*by Rosanne Bittner*

## LATE NIGHT DANCING
*by Diana Silber*

## SUMMER'S KNIGHT
*by Virginia Lynn*

**Ask for them by name.**

*New York Times Bestseller*
## TEXAS! SAGE
*by Sandra Brown*

Winner of every major romance writing award, Sandra Brown is an extraordinary talent whose wonderfully crafted love stories combine tender, unforgettable emotion with breathtaking sensuality. TEXAS! SAGE, the third book in her highly praised TEXAS! trilogy, features the "little" sister of the heroes of the first two books, Lucky and Chase, in a novel that is stormy, moving, and unforgettable.

In the following scene, set on Christmas Day, Sage has just received the worst present of her life—her fiancé, Travis, has just told her the wedding is off. . . .

Stepping away from a column, she wiped the tears off her face, refusing to indulge in them.

First on the agenda was finding a way out of this place. Hell would freeze over before she'd return to the party inside. Taking a deep breath of determination, she turned toward the corner of the veranda.

She took only one step before drawing up short.

He was loitering against the ivy-covered wall, partially hidden in the shadow thrown by a potted evergreen. There was, however, enough light spilling through the windows for Sage to see him well. Too well.

He was tall and lanky, even thinner than her brother Lucky. Although much of his hair was hidden beneath a damp, black felt cowboy hat pulled low over his brows, Sage could see that the hair above his ears was dark blond, shot through with streaks of pale ivory. Long exposure to the outdoors had left him with a deeply baked-on tan and sunbursts radiating from the outer corners of electric blue eyes, which were regarding her with unconcealed amusement.

He had a firm, square jaw that suggested he wasn't to be messed with, and a lean, wiry musculature that justified the arrogant tilt of his head and his insolent stance.

He was wearing a pale blue western shirt, with round, pearl snap buttons. His jeans had a ragged hem. The faded, stringy fringe curled over the instep of his scuffed boots, the toes of which were wet and muddy. His only concession to the chilly evening was a quilted black vest. It was spread open over his shirt because he had the thumbs of both hands hooked into the hip pockets of his jeans.

He was about six feet four inches of broad-shouldered, long-legged, slim-hipped Texan. Bad-boy Texan. Sage despised him on sight, particularly because he seemed on the verge of a burst of laughter at her expense. He didn't laugh, but what he said communicated the same thing.

"Ho-ho-ho. Merry Christmas"

In an attempt to hide her mortification, Sage angrily demanded, "Who the hell are you?"

"Santy Claus. I sent out my red suit to be dry cleaned."

She didn't find that at all amusing. "How long have you been standing there?"

"Long enough," he replied with a grin of the Cheshire cat variety.

"You were eavesdropping."

"Couldn't help it. It would have been rude to bust up such a tender scene."

Her spine stiffened and she gave him an intentionally condescending once-over. "Are you a guest?"

He finally released the laugh that had been threatening. "Are you serious?"

"Then are you part of that?" She indicated the sight-seeing traffic. "Did your car break down or something?"

While shaking his head no, he sized her up and down. "Is that guy queer or what?"

Sage wouldn't deign to retort.

The stranger smacked his lips, making a regretful sound. "The thing is, it'd be a damn shame if you ever got rid of those leather britches, the way they fit you and all."

"How dare—"

"And if you'd squirmed against me the way you were squirming against him, I would have given you the sexiest kiss on record, and to hell with whoever might be looking."

No one, not even her most ardent admirers, had ever had the gall to speak to her like that. If she hadn't shot them herself, her brothers would have. Cheeks flaming, eyes flashing, she told him, "I'm calling the police."

"Now why would you want to go and do that, Miss Sage?" His usage of her name stopped her before she could take more than two steps toward the door. "That's right," he said, reading her mind. "I know your name."

"That's easily explainable," she said with more equanimity than she felt. "While rudely eavesdropping on a conversation that obviously went way over your head, you heard Travis call me by name."

"Oh, I understood everything that was said, all right. Y'all were speaking English. Mama's Boy dumped you, plain and simple. I thought I'd politely wait until he finished before delivering my message to you."

She glared at him with smoldering anger and keen suspicion. "You're here to see *me*?"

"Now you're catching on."

"What for?"

"I was sent to fetch you."

"To fetch me?"

"Fetch you home."

"To Milton Point?"

"That's home, isn't it?" he asked, flashing her a white smile. "Your brother sent me."

"Which one?"

"Lucky."

"Why?"

"Because your sister-in-law, Chase's wife, went into labor t[h]
afternoon."

Up to that point, she'd been playing along with him. She did[n't]
believe a word he said, but she was curious to learn just h[ow]
creative a criminal mind like his could get. To her surprise, he w[as]
privy to family insider information.

"She's in labor?"

"As of two o'clock this afternoon."

"She's not due until after the first of the year."

"The baby made other plans. Didn't want to miss Christma[s, I]
guess. She might have had it by now, but she hadn't when I le[ft.]"

Her wariness remained intact. "Why would Lucky send [you]
after me? Why didn't he just call?"

"He tried. One of your roommates in Austin told him yo[u'd]
already left for Houston with Loverboy." He nodded toward [the]
windows behind which the guests were being ushered into [the]
dining room.

"All things considered," he continued, "Lucky reckone[d it]
would take me less time if I just scooted down here to pick [you]
up." He pushed himself away from the wall, gave the drip[ping]
skies a disparaging glance and asked, "You ready?"

"I'm not going anywhere with you," she exclaimed, scornfu[l of]
his assumption that she would. "I've been driving to and f[rom]
Milton Point since I was eighteen. If I'm needed at home, [my]
family will contact me and—"

"He said you'd probably be a pain in the butt about th[is."]
Muttering and shaking his head with aggravation, he fished [in]
the breast pocket of his shirt and came up with a slip of paper[. He]
handed it to her. "Lucky wrote that for me to give you in case [you]
gave me any guff."

She unfolded the piece of paper and scanned the lines that [had]
obviously been written in a hurry. She could barely read [his]
handwriting, but then no one could read Lucky's handwrit[ing.]
Lucky had identified the man as Tyler Drilling's new emplo[yee,]
Harlan Boyd.

"Mr. Boyd?"

One corner of his lips tilted up. "After all we've been thr[ough]
together, you can call me Harlan."

"I'm not going to call you anything," she snapped. His [smile]
only deepened.

"Lucky offered me fifty bucks to come fetch you."

"Fifty dollars?" she exclaimed.

He tipped back his cowboy hat. "You sound surprised. Do you ̦ure that's too much or too little?"

"All I know is that I'm not going anywhere with you. I'll drive ̦self to Milton Point."

"You can't, remember? You left your car in Austin and drove ̦wn here with Hot Lips." The lines around his eyes crinkled ̦en he smiled. "I guess you could ask him to take you home. ̦though his mama would probably have a conniption fit if her ̦tle boy wasn't home at Christmastime. But you're not going to ̦k him, are you, Miss Sage?"

He knew the answer to that before he asked it, and she hated ̦m for it. Throwing his body weight slightly off-center and ̦laxing one knee, he assumed a stance that was both arrogant and ̦gnacious. His thumbs found a resting place in his hip pockets ̦ce again. "Now, Miss Sage, are you coming peaceably, or are ̦u going to make me work for my fifty dollars?"

She gnawed on her lip. He was correct on several points, ̦iefly that she was stranded at Travis Belcher's house. She ̦asn't about to throw herself upon Travis's mercy. Even though ̦arlan Boyd was a lowlife and her brothers had consigned her to ̦end time with him—something she intended to take up with ̦em at her earliest possible opportunity—her pride wouldn't ̦low her to turn to a single soul in that house.

"I guess you don't leave me much choice, do you, Mr. Boyd?"

"I don't leave you any choice. Let's go."

She tried to go around him, but he sidestepped and blocked her ̦th. Tilting back her head, she glared up at him. It was a long ̦ay up. She had inherited the Tyler height from her daddy, just ̦e her brothers. There were few men she could really look up to. ̦ was disquieting. So was the heat radiating from his eyes. So was ̦s voice, which was soft, yet tinged with masculine roughness ̦d grit.

"Given the chance you gave Loverboy, I'd've lapped you up ̦e a tomcat with a bowl of fresh, sweet cream."

## SONG OF THE WOLF
### by Rosanne Bittner

̦hey called her Medicine Wolf, and she was born at a ̦me when buffalo herds stretched farther than the ̦harpest eye could see—a time when a people called ̦e Cheyenne were a proud and free nation. Across the

windswept plains, the white men were coming to
the land and break a people's spirits—and their he
But fate would bring Medicine Wolf a love so deep
unyielding that nothing on earth could stop it .
passion she would traverse the land to find—and f
the haunting, heartbreaking path of the wolf to ke

Medicine Wolf clung to her father's arm as he walked her
edge of the village, where Bear Paw waited. Bear Paw would
her to the wedding tipi Medicine Wolf and her mother had e
out of sight of the village, along the river, a peaceful, pretty
where they could be alone. It was nearly dark, and at la
would sleep the night in Bear Paw's arms! The thought bro
mixture of anticipation and apprehension. The splendid Bea
would be her husband!

They came closer, and Bear Paw stood next to the white st
he had recently captured from a herd of wild horses. Me
Wolf was sure he had never looked more handsome. He
bleached buckskins, the leggings and fringed shirt beaded
own proud mother, Little Bird. His long, black hair was tied
side of his head, beads woven into it. A bone hairpipe ne
accented the muscles of his neck. Such a magnificent warr
was! She wanted to shout and sing. Could any woman on ea
as happy as she was today?

She watched his eyes fill with pleasure as he looked upo
Yes, today she was a woman. She wore a new white tun
mother had made for her, for she had outgrown the on
Grandmother had made so many years ago. Her wedding
was covered in circular designs of colorful beads, little bell
into the long fringe at the sleeves and hem. Star Woma
worked on the dress for many months, in anticipation c
daughter's marriage.

Medicine Wolf's hair hung long and straight, a bright, b
hairpiece tied into one side. On the belt of her dress she wo
little medicine bag containing the wolf paws, but she wou
need their magic this night to keep her happy.

Black Buffalo stood beside Bear Paw. When Arrow
came close and held out his daughter's hand to her c
husband, Black Buffalo chanted a prayer to *Maheo* to ble
marriage with much love and happiness. Bear Paw took Me
Wolf's hand and could feel her trembling. He squeezed her
more firmly, giving her a smile that told her never to fear
Black Buffalo finished, and Bear Paw captured Me
Wolf's gaze as he spoke his vows.

"Forever I will love you," he told her. "I will provide for you and protect you. Your vision has been mine, and mine, yours. We have been one in heart and spirit for many years. Now we will be one in body."

The words made Medicine Wolf feel hot all over, and she struggled to find her own voice. "And forever I will love you," she responded. "I have loved you since I was but a child and you were part of my vision. I will keep your tipi warm and provide you with many sons who will one day become great warriors like their father."

"It is done," Black Buffalo told them. "Medicine Wolf now belongs to Bear Paw." He gave out a piercing cry, signaling the village.

Medicine Wolf and Bear Paw both smiled as those in the village whooped and shouted in return, expressing their joy. Black Buffalo and Arrow Maker left them. There would be much feasting and celebrating in the village this night, but the newly-weds would not be there. Already they could hear drumming, as Bear Paw took hold of Medicine Wolf and lifted her with ease onto the back of his horse. He mounted up behind her, putting strong arms around her and riding off into a thick grove of trees, toward the wedding tipi.

Finally, after all these years and all their dreams, they belonged to each other. They reached the secret place that belonged only to them, and Bear Paw lifted her down. Everything they needed was here, food, extra clothing, all was prepared. Bear Paw took his straw-filled saddle and the blanket from his horse and tied the animal to a tree. Medicine Wolf waited beside the tipi, her heart pounding, not sure just what he expected of her this first night. Would he understand her secret fears? White Horse's attack had left its stinging memory, had spoiled her vision of what this moment should be.

Bear Paw had said nothing all the way here. He had simply kept one strong arm about her waist, his lips caressing her hair. He came to her now, standing in front of her, drinking in her beauty with his eyes.

Medicine Wolf felt a sudden, overwhelming urge to cry. She struggled against it. What a terrible thing to do on her wedding night! She saw Bear Paw frown at the sight of her quivering lips and misting eyes.

He reached out and touched her face with a big hand. "So," he said, "you think I would just quickly take you for my own pleasure?" He pulled her close, crushing her against him. "I am not White Horse," he told her. "I have waited for this moment for too many years to let it be anything but perfect. No, my wife, will not take you tonight. Tonight I will only hold you." He moved a hand to the shoulders of her tunic, untying the dress. "But I wish to look upon my beautiful wife."

She shivered, and silent tears of joy mixed with anger at herself for crying slid down her cheeks. He stepped back from her slightly, letting the dress fall. She heard him suck in his breath, but she could not bring herself to meet his eyes. Fire ripped through her when he touched a breast with the back of his hand.

"I am greatly honored," he said, his voice gruff with emotion. "Not only is my wife a sacred woman with great powers, but she is also the most beautiful Cheyenne woman who ever walked." He came closer and picked her up in his arms, carrying her inside the tipi.

A morning mist made the broad horizon beyond the river a gentle haze of green and gold, a soft, almost unreal scene. Medicine Wolf stood in front of her wedding tipi, where Bear Paw still slept. It still seemed incredible to her that he had kept his promise and had only held her last night. It was such a sweet, comforting feeling, and she knew she could always trust his word. But now she worried she might have disappointed him by not yet being fully a wife to him.

She walked farther away to pick up some wood for a fire. She should make Bear Paw something to eat. It seemed men were always hungry, or so it was with her father and brother. They would be camped here for one full week, remaining apart from the rest of the village, talking, getting to know each other. This was their special time. They would think only of happy things, and they would try very hard to make a baby. That was most important. She was anxious now for a child of her own, and nothing would make her prouder than to give Bear Paw a son. But that meant she must stop being afraid of mating. Last night her husband had shown her she could trust him. Now she would have to trust him to make a woman of her and not be afraid of the pain.

She turned to go back to the tipi when she saw him standing at the entrance, wearing only his breechcloth. His near-naked splendor almost took her breath away.

She moved closer to him and set down the wood, and she knew by the look in his eyes that he was a man wanting his woman. She told herself she would make him wait no longer. He walked close to her and took her hand. "We are friends, but still we are not overs," he told her softly. "Last night I showed you I make no demands, for I honor you. But you are so beautiful, my wife, and yearn to show you my love in every way."

Medicine Wolf wondered if she might faint. "It is not you that fear," she answered, her voice sounding small and far away. Nor do I fear becoming a woman. The only thing I fear is that I will not please you."

He put a hand to her chin, forcing her to look up at him. "I am our husband now. You can look me in the eyes, Medicine Wolf." he studied his handsome face as he spoke, the straight, white teeth, the true, dark eyes, the way his full lips moved as he spoke. How could you think you might not please me," he asked her. Never have I beheld such beauty. And our hearts have been as ne since you were but a child. Last night we talked of many hings. We know each other's dreams and visions, each other's esires, each other's hearts. All that is left is to know each other's odies. And I promise you, Medicine Wolf, that in not too many ays, perhaps only hours, you will want to share bodies as eagerly nd as often as I. Do you think you are the only one who worries hat you will not please? I, too, want to please you."

She smiled in surprise, her eyes moving over his magnificent rame. "How could you think . . ."

He put a finger to her lips. "Let me make love to you, my wife, efore I die from the want of you. Last night was more painful for ne than any injury I have ever suffered."

She swallowed, realizing it would be almost cruel to tell him o, nor did she want to. There seemed to be fire in his fingertips vhen he touched her shoulders then to untie her tunic. She let it all away from her, and she wondered if he could hear her heart ounding, hoping that her legs would not grow so weak that she ell to the ground. She dropped her eyes again and felt his own yes moving over her in her nakedness.

She was at his mercy now, but it was not like with White Horse. t was beautiful; gentle. He scooped her up in his strong arms as hough she were a mere feather and carried her into the tipi, where ie laid her on their bed of robes. She started to curl up, but he isked her to lie still. His eyes looked watery with a mixture of lesire and near worship. "I have never seen such a beautiful creature," he told her, his own voice strained. He turned and lipped his hands into a wooden bowl of oil his mother had prepared for him, a mixture of water and fragrant oils from the tems of certain flowers. She had put it in a water bag for him, elling him it was good to use to relax his new wife and take away

her fears. He had poured it into the bowl before coming f
Medicine Wolf, determined that before the sun was fully risen,
would have laid his claim to her.

He turned back to her, touching her shoulders with his oile
hands. "Close your eyes and think only of good things," he to
her. "Your muscles are tense, my wife, like mine get before goin
into a battle." He leaned closer, his hair loose now, shrouding h
face as he touched his cheek to hers. "This is not a battle, m
love. This is the most wonderful thing we will ever know."

# LATE NIGHT DANCING
### by Diana Silber

From the acclaimed author of Confessions comes
compelling novel of three friends, sophisticated Lc
Angeles women with busy, purposeful lives, who als
live on the fast track of romance and sex—because, lik
lonely women everywhere, they hunger for a man 
love.

The fast track can be dangerous. . . .

Cassie fights for sleep, but like a defeated, war-weary surviv
she retreats, dragging back to wakefulness. Her eyes reluctant
open. She lies on her back staring up at continents on the ceilir
designed by the sun in a gauzy shimmer through the thin curtain

Seven-thirty! God! Who's mowing the lawn at seven-thirty 
the morning?

A tall stranger in a Raiders T-shirt and well-worn jeans push
the mower across her grass, winnowing neat rows. From th
window Cassie charts the perfectly aligned patterns as she shou
down to the unknown titan, but the roar of the machine swallov
her voice. Finally, cranking the window closed in disgust, sl
pulls on a robe and goes downstairs.

"Hey, who are you?" She has stormed out to the back porch ar
waved him to a stop.

After so much racket the quiet is stunning, and all of a sudde
Cassie feels uncomfortable. She is crinkled from sleep, her sho
blond hair uncombed, her face without the least touch of makeu
She shifts her bare feet on the cool wood. "Who are you?" sl
repeats. "What happened to Yang?"

"I'm working for him now. The name's Jake."

Cassie tugs the robe tighter and folds her arms across her breasts. His blue eyes are flinty, chips of lazulite, and his gaze is unwavering. He doesn't look at her as Yang does, off to the side and unfocused.

"Do you have to start so early? You woke me up." The accusation, sleep-riddled, comes out too harshly. Foolishly she almost apologizes. The anger, grainy and directed at the mower as much as the man—can't they invent quiet machines?—begins to slip away from her. Faced with this Jake, she is somehow at fault. It must be the lost half hour of sleep. Every minute matters. Cassie loves sleep as a fat woman does ice cream. She envies insomniacs their endless nights of interrupted time.

She blames Mandy's going to college a month before for this weariness, but it had been the same when Doug left, three years ago last July. Whenever, in fact, life produces insoluble problems, sleep is the prescription. A stupid antidote; sleep is no solution at all, but an invisible weight will press her shoulders, bend her spine like a straw, as the air clots and she sinks down in her bed, grateful as a lover.

All this, she thinks, for a missed half hour!

Yang's Jake starts the mower again. She turns abruptly and leaves the cut grass blowing behind her.

By the time Cassie comes out again the gardener has gone. His truck no longer nudges its bumper to the curb. A collection of camellias in a tin can sits by the steps. Cassie almost trips over them. A penciled note sticks up between the leaves.

*Sorry.*

A nice gesture, Cassie thinks, carrying the can back into the house. She leaves it on the sink but brings the image of this Jake with her outside and down the steps. She sees the darkness of his eyes and the sweat shining on his upper lip and admonishes herself. Forget him! But he stubbornly clings in her memory.

Eve would tell her why. *Biology, pure and simple,* she hears Eve saying. But who was Eve to tell Cassie about biology? Cassie is the doctor; yet, *ha,* she hears Eve laugh in imaginary conversation, *you treat only women at the clinic and I'm the one who knows about men.* Did she? Did any woman?

Cassie hadn't known about Doug. Just as in magazine stories he came home every night for dinner. He never smelled of musky perfume. No long red or brown or any color but his own blond hair graced his jacket. He made love generously and on cue. Doug even brought her flowers when there was no occasion for gifts, except maybe to mark the stolen lunch hours shared with his lover.

But there weren't all that many roses, not enough for him to pack up and leave, saying, with the pretended grace of a man swept by poetry, *I'm in love with another woman.* Are there any words so brutal? Cassie would banish them, tries to with sleep, but they scar her in hard ridges and wait to greet her on awakening, the first bars of unharmonious dawn. If Cassie isn't careful, Doug's lips repeatedly form the impossible: *another woman.*

On principle she hates Tracy—Doug's lover and new wife— living in glassy sun-splashed splendor in Marina del Rey. Mandy, returning from twice-monthly visits, tells Cassie they aren't happy. Tracy drinks Diet Pepsi for breakfast and listens to Julio Iglesias. Tracy isn't neat. She ignores dishes in the sink and towels on the floor; she trails sand in from the beach. But Cassie recognizes Mandy's reports for the loving messages they are. Tracy is just a woman, *if another.*

Youngish and with a colt's awkwardness the one time she and Cassie met, Tracy is sullen. If she hadn't stolen Cassie's husband she would have captured someone else's. Tracy is a poacher. She displays the heavy-lidded drowsiness of a female too lazy to do her own legitimate hunting.

Cassie thinks too often of Doug. Not only in the first flush of shock and bereavement when, wounded, she stumbled, wept, invented heresies to believe in, but afterward. She recuperates because that is what women do when their men betray them; otherwise they are pitiful creatures, victims of those stubborn infections that won't respond to treatment. Cassie agrees with her well-wishers that Doug is a shit, better off forgotten, not worth a tear, a moment's unsound sleep. Not that her sleep is interrupted by Doug, by any marauder. Her sleep is medicinal. She should have given up the excess hours long since—oh, yes, she knows she is, in a manner of speaking, narcoleptic—and the dark dirges of unconsciousness. But she wants him back, not for himself but to eradicate the bludgeon of rejection, to be vindicated. A returning husband removes the stain of abandonment.

The Magdalene Clinic is south of National, a jigsaw-puzzle area of middle class and blue collar. A gynecologist-obstetrician, a woman's doctor, Cassie lives a life given to secrets. The words *breasts, uterus, cervix, ovaries, Fallopian tubes, vulva, vagina,* have everyday value for her, as do, among others, *dysmenorrhea, conception, pregnancy, abortion, hysterectomy.* There are so many diseases and conditions women endure that are foreign to men, so many malfunctions of their peculiar organs. The design of the female, though miraculous, is imperfect. She knows hersel the pain of childbirth, PMS, the breathless waiting for the late stain on her panties. Faced with fluttering eyelids and sweaty hands, she explains the intricacies of birth control and wonders if the propagation of the species couldn't have been achieved in a more humane fashion. Why are women the bearers of the entire burden?

Despite Doug and the reality of her work, Cassie doesn't hate men. That would have been as foolish as loathing dogs because one bit her and others barked and leaped up with muddy paws. Men are only the opposite, the left to right, anodes to cathodes. They are just of a simpler construction.

All the physicians and nurses in the clinic are women, perhaps not deliberately—they know too much about sexual discrimination to practice it themselves, they promise one another—but they haven't sought out males either. There are Harry Bryan in administration and Chris Tomlan, the staff accountant, and some of the cleaning crew are male; but basically Magdalene is a woman's domain. Cassie spends her days in the world of females.

How do you think you'll ever find a man? Eve demands, brushing away Cassie's I'm-not-looking.

Eve, Cassie's best friend, is in real estate, a much more male-oriented field, as she puts it, which is lucky for someone married three times and constantly auditioning future husbands. Eve's hunger for mates border on the ridiculous, but she shrugs off Cassie's criticism by saying *Such is nature*. Men aren't necessary for every female at all times, Cassie counters in their running argument. She has had hers, plus marriage, a child. So what if there will be no long glide into twilight, days of gray hair and rocking chairs, the retirement porch of shuffling memories. She is certainly better off than her other close friend Nona, six months shy of forty and panicking, her biological clock ticking as loudly as a timer on dynamite.

The phone rings as Cassie buttons her white coat. It is Eve to remind her of dinner at seven. "You're driving. Okay? But tell me, before I hang up—met any good men?"

"Since I talked to you yesterday?"

"Well, miracles are known to occur. You could have bumped fenders with Sylvester Stallone. He's single, at least momentarily."

She has no time for Eve's teasing. "I have patients waiting."

"And I have a house weeping to be sold."

Men. She is getting as bad as Eve, catching herself as she go
through the day wondering whom she might meet. What is this,
sea change, a strange scent on the wind? Like Mandy, is sl
tricking herself into forgetting?

## SUMMER'S KNIGHT
### by Virginia Lynn

A New Orleans heiress, Summer St. Clair never dreame
that fleeing from an arranged marriage would leave he
stranded, penniless and alone, in the unfamiliar stree
of London. But her terrifying ordeal soon turned int
breathtaking adventure when she captured the glitte
ing eyes of an untamed rogue. In the following e:
cerpt, Summer finds an unexpected savior in a shabl
inn. . . .

"Are you, by any chance, on your way to London, sir?"

He wasn't. He'd intended to avoid the city completely; but now
looking at this wide-eyed girl with the slightly tilted eyes a
winsome smile, he hesitated in saying so.

He sat and watched the girl for a moment. He toyed with tl
idea of seduction. She looked luscious. Her hair was an odd col
when dry, with thick strands of varying shades of gold alternati
with darker tints of brown, as if she had been in the sun a gre
deal. But her complexion proved that she could not have lingere
in the sun; it was pale and creamy, without a single blemisl
except perhaps, for one or two freckles dusting the end of h
straight little nose. She had high cheekbones and a full, sult:
mouth; her eyes were wide, thick-lashed, unusually blue, a dee
color that made him think of summer bluebells.

Jamie sighed. She was beautiful. Really beautiful.

"Yes," he heard himself say, "I am traveling in that directio
Why?"

"Would it be possible for me to travel along with you?"

It was impossible to refuse. He smiled. "Of course."

Summer hesitated, then added in a soft, urgent voice, "I'm
something of a hurry, sir."

"Are you?" His dark gaze riveted on her mouth, and l
wondered if her lips tasted as luscious as they looked. "Why a
you in a hurry, lass?"

Jamie's gaze snapped back to her eyes when she said, "I must meet a ship before it sails."

"A ship?" His brow lowered slightly. "What ship?"

"The *Sea Dancer*. You see, I came over from America on her, and if I can just reach London before she sails again, I will be able to return home."

Her words were fast, running into one another so that he had a little difficulty in following them, but somehow, it was what she *didn't* say that interested him most.

Leaning forward, he clasped his hands on the top of the table. "How will you buy passage if you have no money?"

Summer hesitated a shade too long before saying, "The captain is a . . . *friend*."

"Ah. A *friend*." He thought he understood. Of course she would have a protector. Any female who traveled with an unreliable maid and a small cloth bag holding only a few items of clothing could not be as well-bred as he'd first thought. A pity. Or was it? If she was not some convent-bred miss from a fine family, it certainly left the door open to seduction.

Summer recognized from his expression what he thought and opened her mouth to explain. Then she shut it again. Why not let him think that she had a lover? It might save her from what she saw in his eyes if he thought she was already spoken for.

She met his gaze steadily. "I'm not exactly naive, sir. I know what I'm about in life, if you understand."

That single black brow rose, and he nodded silently, seeming to digest this bit of information as she had wished him to do.

"Do you have enough money to pay the coach fare for both of us? I have a necklace that we could sell, perhaps, if you don't. . . ."

Startled by her assumption of his inability to pay, he started to correct her, then paused. It had been a few years since he'd had to live off his wits; it might amuse him to do so for a while now. Especially since it would put him in the position of gallant cavalier to a young lady in distress. It wouldn't hurt the seduction he planned at all. In fact, he found he liked the idea quite well.

"Don't barter your necklace yet," he said. "I think I have enough to pay our way."

"Good. When we reach London, I will see to it that you are repaid for your kindness," Summer said earnestly, and saw an amused light flare in her benefactor's eyes.

"Will you, lass?"

She seemed surprised. "Of course."

A smile flickered at the corners of his mouth, and his voice was deliberately husky. "I won't charge highly for my services, lass. Just a simple kiss will be payment enough."

"A simple kiss?" Summer echoed, sensing that with this man who fairly radiated male vitality and virility, there would be no such thing. She bludgeoned her quickening pulse into submission before saying coolly, "I find your suggestion vulgar and shocking, sir!"

"Come, lass—it will be such a small thing to do for a man willing to put himself out to escort you safely to London, don't you think?"

Summer thought it over for several moments, then knew she had little choice. "Very well," she said with the air of a martyr, "I accept your terms. One kiss, and no more, and you will take me to the port of London."

"You may not want to stop at a single kiss," he said. "Have you thought of that?"

"Not at all." She glared at him for a moment, then gave a soft sigh. "I'm ready," she said, and leaned across the table. She closed her eyes and put up her face for his kiss, tensing against it. In spite of herself, her pursed lips tingled with anticipation as she waited for him to kiss her.

Jamie stared at her. "I've no intention of kissing you here in the middle of the common room with the innkeeper and half his staff watching us. I'll collect my payment when I'm ready."

Summer's eyes snapped open, and she felt very foolish. Her high cheekbones reddened, and her mobile lips tightened into a line. She'd not thought of that. But perhaps he had the better idea, especially when she noted the faintly malicious, watchful eyes peering at them from across the room.

She nodded stiffly, and the quick glance she gave him was eloquent. "Agreed, sir."

Jamie watched her with veiled eyes, knowing what must be going through her mind. She was right. He did want her. His body ached with the wanting; he shifted uncomfortably. It should be a fair enough trade. She wanted to go to London; he wanted to bury himself inside her.

She rose from the chair, then, struck by a thought, she looked at him. "By the by—what is your name?"

His dark brow quirked in amusement. "Ah, so you've grown curious about me, have you? James Douglas Cameron, at your service," he said with a sweeping bow. "And I love a challenge, lass. It makes victory all the sweeter."

# FANFARE

## Now On Sale
### *New York Times* Bestseller
# TEXAS! SAGE
☐ (29500-4) $4.99/5.99 in Canada
### by Sandra Brown

*The third and final book in Sandra Brown's beloved TEXAS! trilogy.
Sage Tyler always thought she wanted a predictable, safe man . . . until a
lean, blue-eyed drifter takes her breath, and then her heart away.*

# SONG OF THE WOLF
☐ (29014-2) $4.99/5.99 in Canada
### by Rosanne Bittner

*Young, proud, and beautiful, Medicine Wolf possesses extraordinary
healing powers and a unique sensitivity that leads her on an unforgettable
odyssey into a primeval world of wildness, mystery, and passion.*

# LATE NIGHT DANCING
☐ (29557-8) $5.99/6.99 in Canada
### by Diana Silber

*A compelling novel of three friends -- sophisticated Los Angeles women with
busy, purposeful lives, who also live on the fast track of romance and sex,
because, like lonely women everywhere, they hunger for a man to love.*

# SUMMER'S KNIGHT
☐ (29549-7) $4.50/5.50 in Canada
### by Virginia Lynn

*Heiress Summer St. Clair is stranded penniless on the streets of London,
but her terrifying ordeal soon turns to adventure when she captures the
glittering eyes of the daring Highland rogue, Jamie Cameron.*

☐ Please send me the books I have checked above. I am enclosing $ _____ (add $2.50 to cover
postage and handling). Send check or money order, no cash or C. O. D.'s please.

Mr./ Ms. _____

Address _____

City/ State/ Zip _____

Send order to: Bantam Books, Dept. FN, 414 East Golf Road, Des Plaines, IL 60016

Please allow four to six weeks for delivery.

Prices and availability subject to change without notice.

## THE SYMBOL OF GREAT WOMEN'S
## FICTION FROM BANTAM

Ask for these books at your local bookstore or use this page to order.

FN27 - 3/92